Small Town Secrets

WELCOME TO SEA PORT
BOOK THREE

KATRINA JACKSON

Editor: A.K. Edits

Cover artist: Celia Moscote

Cover designer: Katrina Jackson

To me and every girl I loved in my youth-

Thanks for teaching me that it can always get messier. It was probably worth it in the end.

Map Legend

1. Perv Place
2. Santos's house
3. Freedom and Waltham farms
4. Douglass Park
5. Sully and Willie's duplex
6. Confections
7. Mary/Lorraine's cottage
8. The Grove
9. Knox's apartment
10. Sully's
11. Sunnyside Diner
12. Jonah's house
13. Sea Port Administrative Building*
14. Orange Grove County Library
15. La Bella Rosa
16. Bria's house

   *containing the Firehouse, Mayor's Office, Police Precinct, and Post Office

Content Warnings

Allusions to past infidelity
Grief (parental death)

WELCOME TO SEA PORT

Prologue

LORRAINE

Lorraine shuffled into the kitchen of her and Jonah's new house, half-asleep and still a little sore from the night before. It was only muscle memory that made it possible for her to grind some beans and get the drip coffee machine going. If she'd had to think too hard about any part of her morning routine, she'd still be staring at her brand-new kitchen in complete confusion. Now, at least she could stare into space while waiting for her coffee to brew. She was facing the big, bright window above the kitchen sink, staring at the side of Mary's house across their shared yard, but she wasn't seeing anything, not really. Not the wet, dewy grass or the gray sky, because her brain was too busy working.

She hadn't gotten much sleep last night — and only some of that was Jonah's fault. The Orange Grove County Read-a-thon started today. Bringing the reading challenge back to Sea Port was Willie's bright idea, even against Lorraine's professional objections. Lorraine loved the program in theory, but she'd tried to convince Willie to let another library host it this first year — or three — at least until they had a few dozen more kids enrolled in Sea Port schools. It was a good recommendation, but in hindsight, Lorraine could see how it had failed.

For all Willie's efforts to rebuild their town one new Transplant at a time, their demographics were skewed. Apparently, there was a never-ending fount of single people ready to leave their old lives behind and move themselves — and maybe their pets — to the middle of nowhere. Shockingly, people with kids were much less adventurous, especially considering the diminished state of the Sea Port public school system. Who knew? It wasn't that Sea Port schools were bad; they just needed a little TLC, just like every other part of town. It was a testament to how much people loved Sea Port that they worked with the school to give their kids the best education they could and Lorraine wanted to support that work, but she was only one person.

For her part, Willie had listened to Lorraine's advice and she took some of it, which is why Lorraine was launching the read-a-thon event for all ages. Sometimes it was just easier to follow Willie's lead. She was the mayor after all.

For weeks, Lorraine had been designing and printing bingo cards and driving around the county looking for prize donations for reader rewards — free appetizers at La Bella Rosa, a dozen free cookies of your choice from Confections, a couple dozen eggs from one of the outer farms, dinner at the Sunnyside, a free lap dance at the Dusty Pearl in Parkdale. Lorraine had been running herself ragged making sure there was a prize for every type of reader they might encounter.

At the end of the day, all that mattered to Lorraine was

that every program they organized pulled people through the doors of their brand-new library. She was willing to do almost anything. She even had a running list of programming ideas in her cellphone and didn't care how long it took to cross them all off. Sea Port was her new home and she — and Jonah — had nothing but time.

She was a full-on convert to Willie's mission to grow their little town, even if it ran her just a little bit ragged.

"You plotting world domination or tryna remember if you shut the lights out in the library last night?" Jonah asked.

"Both," Lorraine said, blinking back into the moment. She reached for her coffee cup but came up empty. She frowned down at the counter and then looked at the coffee pot, surprised to find it still full.

Jonah came up behind her and kissed her shoulder. "How long you been standing here?" he asked gently.

"No idea. I'm nervous," she admitted in a whisper.

He wrapped his arms around her waist. "About the read-a-thon?"

"Yeah. What if no one comes? Or what if they come but no one reads? Or what if I run out of prizes?"

Lorraine had spent the last few weeks planning today's opening reception. She'd been working with their neighbors to get people visiting as many of the county's libraries as possible, but Sea Port had Confections cookies and Sully's coffee, so holding their opening event here was a no-brainer. Hopefully.

Jonah laughed into the side of her neck and kissed her skin. "They'll come. You're overthinking it."

"What's new?"

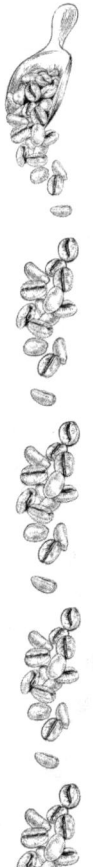

"Good point. I stopped by the Sunnyside yesterday and Terra told me she had a list of books to read already. She wants to win whatever the first-place prize is."

"It's a tablet," Lorraine said.

Jonah kissed his way up to her chin. "She'll like that." His hands started moving over her stomach.

"But it can't just be her," Lorraine said, inching her feet apart.

"It won't be. There ain't nothing these old people like to do more than read and gossip. You know that." Jonah slipped his hand into her boxer shorts, caressing her warm skin as his hand slid down her right thigh.

"Sure, but what about people from the other towns?" she asked in a soft huff of a voice.

"You can't control the other towns, just like you can't control whether or not WAKC takes over the only meeting room in the library for their afternoon knitting session."

Lorraine grunted a soft breath of air at the reminder that she needed to make a sign-up sheet for the meeting rooms ASAP; WAKC meetings were getting out of hand.

"Still no panties," he mumbled as his hand moved between her legs.

"Who wears panties to bed?"

"Not you, thank god," he said as his cool hand inched toward her pussy. She slid her feet apart to make room for him. Jonah's fingers brushed the hood over her clit and they both shivered. He pressed his body tight against her back, his boxers doing nothing to hide his arousal, especially not when he was grinding against her from behind.

Lorraine closed her eyes while Jonah circled her clit in

slow, lazy circles. "Stop teasing me," she moaned. "I need to get to work."

"You got time. Ain't even had your coffee yet," he reminded her as his fingers caressed her wet lips, pulling small groans from both their mouths.

"I don't have time," Lorraine whined, circling her hips on his fingers before letting out a sigh of defeat. "I'll just stop by Sully's on the way."

"You got time," Jonah laughed, trapping her between his body and the counter. Lorraine grunted in frustration while he teased her lips open with his middle finger.

"You don't know my schedule," she moaned.

She could feel Jonah's smile against her cheek. "Yeah, I do," he whispered, just as his middle finger dipped inside her.

"How? I didn't— Oh, fuck." His finger didn't dip in this time. No, this time Jonah pushed deep inside her and started rubbing soft circles over her G-spot. Lorraine's knees went weak and she happily let Jonah hold her upright.

"You shared your calendar with me," he reminded her, moving a second finger through her wetness. It was loud as hell in their quiet kitchen.

"I'd never," she moaned. "Would I?"

"I asked right before I ate you out on your desk," Jonah replied with a bright smile.

"Which time?"

"I'll remind you," he said and then loosened his hold on her.

"No, wait, I believe you," she whined as he pulled his fingers from her pussy. "Wait."

But Jonah didn't wait. Instead, he moved a firm hand up her back and bent her over the kitchen sink while he crouched down behind her. That wiped the frown from Lorraine's face. He pulled her boxers down her legs, his rough hands moving over Lorraine's soft skin. He caressed the back of her thighs before palming both ass cheeks, pulling them apart.

"You have time," Jonah whispered, kissing her left cheek.

Lorraine lifted onto the balls of her feet, arching her back for him. "You're right," she said, swallowing a moan as he laughed against her perineum and then moved down to her wet lips.

She wasn't actually convinced she had time for this at all, but if Jonah wanted to start his day by eating her pussy from the back in their new house, she wasn't going to be the one to stop him.

They'd both be late for work.

SANTOS

Santos was up, dressed, and in the kitchen making coffee before Knox and Mary even crawled out of bed.

He heard them slowly come into consciousness while he sat at the kitchen table, skimming through the newest edition of the *Sea Port Sentinel*, which was pretty boring this week; not nearly enough gossip. It took a herculean effort not to strip out of his uniform and dive back into bed when he heard Mary and Knox come awake for real. Santos had a packed day and couldn't be late, not even for them.

"You're still here?" Mary cried as soon as she walked into the kitchen.

She was wearing a thin floral silk robe tied loosely at the waist. She might as well have been wearing nothing, as thin and short as that robe was. It was Santos's favorite thing in Mary's closet because it didn't hide a single one of her curves and it was coming apart as she walked. She had a relaxed smile on her face. Santos envied that early morning ease.

The sun wasn't even fully above the horizon and his shoulders were already tight with stress. "I am," he said softly.

Mary was on her way to the coffee machine, but she turned back toward him at the sound of his voice. He took a sip of coffee as she moved behind his chair and started massaging his shoulders. "If we'd known, we would've made you come back to bed," she purred, kissing his cheek.

Santos closed his eyes and enjoyed the gentle press of Mary's fingers digging into his shoulders. It wasn't exactly what he wanted, but he wouldn't ever complain about her touching him. "I heard you two," he whispered, "but I can't be late for work today."

Mary sucked her teeth in annoyance. "You can be a little late," she whispered against his ear, her tongue following her words.

He groaned when she sucked his earlobe into her mouth. "I've got a stack of applications to go through."

"Can't Willie do that?" Mary asked, kissing the edge of his beard.

"I don't want to get in the habit of Willie staffing my department."

Her hands stopped moving and she bent forward to kiss his cheek. "Your department," she whispered excitedly. Santos turned his head and kissed Mary's smile softly.

"What'd I miss?" he whispered.

Mary pecked at the corner of his mouth. "Knox almost made my knees touch my shoulders."

"Almost?"

"See why we needed you?" she sighed into his mouth.

Santos lifted his hand and cupped the back of her head, digging his fingers into her soft, messy curls as they kissed. Their tongues slid together making Santos wish he *had* joined them earlier. He'd enjoyed listening to their moans as soothing and arousing white noise while he read through the paper and drowned his stress in caffeine, but it wasn't the same.

Santos had been happier in the last two years of his life than at any time in the decade before, but sometimes he still struggled to believe that this was the life he got to live. That he was really this fucking happy. And horny, but that was just part of the happiness as far as he was concerned.

Thankfully, Mary seemed to think her primary job in their relationship was to make sure their house was a very happy and naked home. "We can try again when you get back from work tonight," she said.

"I'm looking forward to it."

Mary bounced back up and started massaging his shoulders again. "Just think about DPing me when you get bored during your interviews," she said happily.

"No," Santos laughed. "Absolutely not."

Mary shrugged. "Your loss. Is that Lorraine?"

Santos followed Mary's line of sight out the window and across the side lawn they shared with their only neighbors. On a good day, apparently, they could see straight into their neighbors' kitchen, which was how he spotted Lorraine bent over their kitchen counter, eyes closed and mouth open on a silent scream. They couldn't see Jonah, but Santos could guess what he was doing and turned away.

"Mary," he said in a warning tone. His muscles had just started to relax under her touch, but they tensed again. "Mary, stop looking."

"Why? It makes them happy."

"They look really happy without us," Santos said.

"Who's happy without us?" Knox asked with faint scorn in his voice. He walked into the kitchen with a bright pink towel wrapped low and tight around his waist.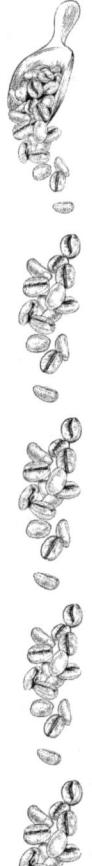

New muscles in Santos's body started tightening.

"Lorraine and Jonah," Mary answered as Knox sidled up to Santos's side. The warm vanilla smell of Mary's body wash filled Santos's nose. He tried to fidget in his seat, but she pressed down on his shoulders, holding him in place.

Santos swallowed a moan. The first of many, probably.

"What do you mean?" Knox asked, bending forward to look out the window. His hard abs hit Santos's shoulder and rested there. "Oh. Well, that's a nice way to start the day." He clapped a hand onto Santos's chest. "You should take notes, Marine."

"Oh, don't tease him," Mary said. "He's still doing interviews. He's busy."

Knox sucked his teeth but bent over and pressed his face into Santos's hair, kissing the crown of his head, before turning away. "We didn't move to Sea Port to work ourselves to death."

The absurdity of that statement pulled Santos out of the haze of lust to defend himself. "It's one morning," he said to Knox's chiseled back.

"That's how it starts," Knox replied with a small sigh.

Mary wrapped her arms loosely around Santos's neck. "Then it's a good thing Santos has us to keep him from overworking." She kissed her way across his cheek and licked the corner of his mouth while they both watched Knox pour himself a cup of coffee.

"I do," he whispered, turning his head and kissing Mary, his eyes still on Knox's back.

He couldn't be too late, but maybe he had a few minutes to spare.

WELCOME TO SEA PORT

ONE

Sully

L isa Sullivan had been in Sea Port for close to four years. Technically, she was the first Transplant to move to town and there were a few Porties who blamed her — and Willie — for the slow, trickling invasion of outsiders ever since. It didn't matter that she'd moved to town nearly half a year before the Sea Port Relocation Initiative even launched or that the program was Willie's baby and Sully was just along for the ride. Small-town gossips didn't care about the truth and Sully only cared that her nosy neighbors spilled their tea in her coffee shop — figuratively speaking. It took a while to settle in a town this small, but after four years, Sully could hardly remember her life before Sea Port, especially now that her café was finally open and busier every day.

She woke up every morning in the duplex she and Willie shared at six on the dot. There were beans to roast and deliveries to sort before she even unlocked the front doors. The best thing about Sea Port was how predictable it could be.

On Fridays, Sully knew to expect Lorraine just after lunch to pick up coffee for her and Jonah. On Mondays, just before City Council meetings, Knox and Santos usually sat in a corner booth talking and laughing, their fingers wrapped around cups of coffee they rarely finished before they trudged across the street for their least favorite meeting. Saturdays were a free-for-all, but Sully could always count on the Wrights showing up as soon as she opened. Sully loved to make their coffees personally and drop them off at that same corner booth. The couple enjoyed watching the town come to life in silence, Mr. Wright lovingly stroking his wife's misshapen and fragile, arthritic hands.

It was a hard sell at first, but Sully had come to adore her new life more than words could express.

Before moving to Sea Port, Sully had been barely surviving the junior executive path at a large regional bank — a job she hated. It wasn't the life she wanted for herself, but it paid the bills and that mattered more than Sully liked to admit. If not for Willie, Sully probably would've stayed in Chicago, met a nice woman, and hated her job every day until she quit or got fired, whichever came first. But when Willie decided to move back to Sea Port, Sully impulsively decided to follow. They'd been roommates and best friends since college. Willie was as much Sully's home as the house she grew up in. Giving up life in a city like Chicago to move to Sea Port was drastic, but when Sully's manager had passed her over for a promotion she'd rightfully earned, what had once been a difficult decision was easier than breathing.

Some people's lives changed slowly over time — one devastating disappointment after another — but Sully's had changed at the speed of light. She'd applied for a business loan and been approved. She and Willie had loaded their apartment into a moving truck and set off on the road for a point on the map Sully still couldn't find, even after all this time. She'd second-guessed herself for weeks until she realized she was fighting a battle she'd already won. Once she realized that, it was easy to start making Sea Port her own, which required fighting other battles, like how to get the locals to treat her like one of their own.

After four years, most Porties still treated Sully like a guest — a guest they liked but still watched from the corner of their eyes, just in case. Compared to some of the other Transplants, Sully was practically a local. But having a job that didn't require regular lunchtime breakdowns was the real win. A busy café and a predictable schedule were icing on the cake — the cake made by Confections, naturally.

But Sea Port was anything but boring. Since the town's professional gossips, the Wednesday Afternoon Knitting Club (WAKC) met in her shop, Sully was accidentally privy to snippets of other people's business she heard while refreshing pots of tea, coffee, and cookies. It was none of her business, but she listened all the same.

Ears open, lips shut wasn't the WAKC motto for nothing.

The Wednesday Afternoon Knitting Club members took over two four-top tables in the center of the dining room almost as soon as Sully's opened each Wednesday, ushered inside by the few teenagers in town — who pronounced the club's acronym as *whack*. They dropped the knitters off in the morning and returned promptly at three to ferry them home. It was a cute little set-up that Sully had welcomed since WAKC members enthusiastically told reluctant Porties that Sully's coffee was the best they'd ever had. Obviously.

Sully had gotten familiar with the rhythms of WAKC's gossip quickly, using their observations to stay informed since they met with more regularity than the *Sentinel* updated their website. Over the last few years, Mary, Knox, and Santos had been the hottest topic of conversation. The Knitting Club had devoted innumerable hours trying to decipher just what in the hell was going on between the baker, the fire chief, and the chief of police. Even now that everyone knew what was going on between those three, WAKC was trying to figure out who exactly was the center of their little triangle. Old Ms. Kemp had decided that Mary and Santos were fighting over Knox because, "Have you seen that man's smile?" and she refused all other opinions.

But then the sightings started. Or maybe near-sightings was more accurate. It seemed like half the town had almost caught the new librarian and Jonah Brown doing something untoward in public, but never in the act. Clothes askew, lipstick smears, shirts buttoned incorrectly, pants not buttoned at all. There was something happening with those two and WAKC was on the case, but much more casually because, "Jonah's been through the ringer. His daddy'd want him to be happy," Mrs. Crawford said empathetically. "And I was young once," she added with a loud cackle after someone mentioned seeing Jonah and Lorraine sneaking into the library garden well after it was closed. Mr. Thornton, the only male member of the group, was less interested in what those two were doing than where, so he'd slipped a town map into his craft bag so they could mark the sightings, always looking for a pattern.

"No one's seen them at the clinic," Mr. Thornton offered while Sully set a sugar-free cranberry muffin in front of him. "You think Wes is haunting that place?"

The group wasn't above paranormal gossip, and that one question had sent them into a tizzy for the rest of the afternoon. Sully liked all her regulars, but WAKC were her favorites — a bit nutty, but very entertaining.

The only time she didn't enjoy WAKC Wednesdays was when they returned to their favorite topic: comparing Mayor Waltham, the Younger, to her inimitable and excessively popular father, Mayor Waltham the Elder, also known as Leroy "Skip" Waltham.

Sully tuned out all Waltham talk as a matter of course. She knew the former Mayor Waltham, but not enough to have an opinion. When people mentioned Mayor Waltham, she only ever thought of Willie, even if she refused to use her title. She was Willie when they met in freshman orientation and she'd be Willie until the day they died. Hell, if she decided to run for governor, Sully would still call her Willie. She'd call her best friend — the girl who'd gotten drunk and thrown up in the middle of their dorm room freshman *and* sophomore years and then wailed her apologies while sitting fully clothed on the shower room floor as Sully cleaned up her mess — 'Mayor' on the fifteenth of never.

Willie was Sully's family, and maybe that's why it took her so long to realize that she was acting strangely. Something was going on with her best friend and Sully was determined to figure out what — hopefully before WAKC beat her to it.

"You look like you're thinking about killin' somebody," Keith said, sidling up next to her behind the cash register.

Sully frowned and turned to find one of her two employees looking at her with confusion etched into the space between his eyebrows.

She'd been the café's only employee for the first year, when every cup of drip coffee had her worried it would be her last. In her second year, success had seemed less like the number in her ledger and more like the ability to hire someone to help her out. Keith started part-time and gave Sully her first midweek day off in months. She'd love him forever for that, but he still got on her nerves.

"Am I paying you to talk smack or work?"

His adorable chubby cheeks lifted with his smile. "Thankfully, I give you the smack for free. A little perk to thank you for the job," he said, shrugging before turning back to the dishes he was washing. The actual job Sully paid him to do.

She would *love* to fire him — or at least threaten to do so — but Keith was the only person who knew how to make the sandwich board sign look pretty and he knew it. All her leverage was gone.

"When you're done with the dishes, you can head to the back and move those sacks of beans," she said.

"Fine," he sighed dramatically.

Just then, the front door opened and Sully turned toward it with a smile on her face — the one she was still perfecting, bright and open but not too friendly. Jonah was holding the door open for Lorraine, but instead of walking inside, she'd pressed herself against him and lifted onto the balls of her feet, their faces inching close for a kiss. Over the last few months, Sully had learned to never look too closely at Lorraine and Jonah unless she wanted one of them to accidentally flash her and force her to add a pin to Mr. Thornton's map, so she shook her head and stepped to the side, ready to tell them to get a room.

Keith beat her to it. "Close the door!" he yelled across the coffee shop. "You're letting all the cool air out."

Jonah let the door go just as Lorraine pulled his mouth to hers.

"Alright, I'll help with the beans later," Sully told Keith.

"Thank goodness," he muttered. "Those bitches are heavy as hell."

"Sorry about that," Lorraine trilled as she bounced inside. "It's such a beautiful day today." Sully and Keith stared at her. "What? It is."

"Maybe for you," Keith muttered. "We're not getting our backs blown out."

"You want your usual, Lorraine?" Sully asked, moving the conversation along.

"Yes, please. Can I get a blueberry muffin also? I'm starving. Didn't have time to eat breakfast this morning."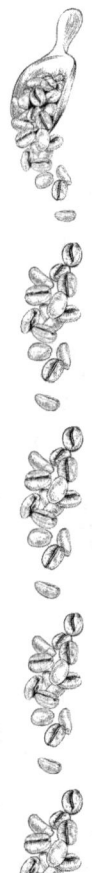

Keith sucked his teeth and glared at Lorraine before drying his hands on a towel.

"What? I could've overslept," she said as he stalked around the counter, snatching the sandwich board leaning against the wall to set it outside again. "I could have!" she called after him.

"You didn't, though," Sully said, punching Lorraine's order into the cash register. "Don't rub your happiness in our single faces."

"You're right," Lorraine giggled, reaching out to grab Sully's left wrist. "But I've never been this happy. I'm starting to think there's something in the water."

Sully sighed. "We're actually out of blueberry muffins. They were popular this morning. You want banana nut?"

Lorraine snatched her hand back. "No. What do you mean, you're out?"

"Calm down," Sully said.

Lorraine took a deep breath and brushed her braids back from her forehead. "It's fine. I'll stop by Confections after this."

"The blueberry muffins are a café exclusive, remember?"

Lorraine's eyes went wide. "No. Absolutely not."

Sully's deal with Mary's bakery had been very financially advantageous for them both. The town liked Sully's coffee but they were obsessed with Mary's confections, even if they were confused about her relationship, and the two women were slowly working to corner the market — literally, since their shops were around the corner from one another. They were moving into the second phase of their partnership with Confections by Mary, exclusive to Sully's. They were still working out the kinks, but for the hardcore sugar addicts, their deal was a success.

Lorraine's face was etched with shock and pain, imploring Sully to fix this problem immediately.

Sully rolled her eyes and checked her watch. "If you can hang around, we should get another drop in a few minutes."

"Oh, perfect," Lorraine said happily, pulling her wallet from her purse. "You should have just said that. Make it two muffins, please."

"I'll get started on your latte," Sully sighed.

"Thanks so much."

Lorraine stepped to the side to wait for her drink while Sully turned toward the espresso machine. A few moments later, she slid Lorraine's drink across the counter. She glanced around the room quickly, but when no one seemed to need anything, she ducked into the back to get ready.

The back of the café was one large storeroom with her coffee roasting machine set prominently in the center. There were bags of fresh beans neatly labeled and stacked to the left, paper cups and lids organized on shelves to the right, and boxes waiting to be broken down and recycled shoved into a corner, but she shimmied past all that to get to the rear of the building where she closed herself in the small employee bathroom. She washed her hands and face, pulled her hair down from the bun she wore just about every day, tried to fluff some life back into her sad curls, considered putting it back in the bun, fluffed it some more, decided she needed lip gloss, realized she didn't have any, and then gave up, pulling her hair back into the bun as usual.

"Maybe today?" she whispered to her reflection, trying to sound hopeful. But then her face fell because she knew the answer was no.

Sully checked the time on her watch. It was a quarter to eleven. By now, Bria would be on her way. Even just thinking her name had Sully's heart hammering against her chest. Would she talk to Bria beyond basic shop talk this morning? Probably not. Would she soak up the few moments when they shared the same air? Absolutely.

Sully wasn't really the kind of person who developed crushes easily, especially not when there was work to do — and there was always work to do — so her feelings for Bria had crept up on her. One second, Bria was Keith's friend, Mary's assistant, a cute girl, and the next, Sully was living for the two deliveries Bria dropped off each week. She literally set aside time to bask in Bria's presence and today was no different.

"Almost time," she whispered excitedly, slowly retracing her steps through the storage room.

Keith was back behind the counter and she tapped his left shoulder, sending him off to buss tables. It was a calculated move to make sure Sully was at the register when Bria arrived and she didn't care. Keith was Bria's best friend; he got to talk to her every day. She only had a few minutes each week to monopolize Bria's attention and she wouldn't sacrifice it for anyone.

Sully thought she'd been doing a damn good job hiding her crush, even if sometimes the thought of Bria's smooth almond-colored skin, the almost-dimple on her left cheek, and those dark eyes made her blush. Maybe more than sometimes. But Sully didn't have many indulgences in life, so she allowed herself to luxuriate in this crush, cataloging her facial expressions, new hairstyles, and clothes as a kind of pathetic gift to herself. She took Bria in entirely, but only for those few minutes.

This had been Sully's pattern for the last year, but then something changed.

Two months ago, Willie had started showing up at Sully's every Wednesday for a cup of tea, always just before Bria arrived, and this morning was the same. The bell over the door chimed as she walked inside. Sully dropped two of Willie's favorite peach ginseng tea bags into a cup and filled it with hot water. They normally chatted for at least a few moments, but on Wednesdays, Willie grabbed her tea, shoved a ten-dollar bill in the tip jar — since Sully refused to take her money — and then turned to the high bar table along the front window to sip her drink in silence.

The allegedly very busy Mayor of tiny, little Sea Port settled into her seat while Sully, the also allegedly hard-working and intrepid businesswoman, wiped a towel over her already-clean counter, both women waiting patiently for Bria to arrive.

Apparently.

For weeks, this situation had alarm bells sounding in Sully's head, but she didn't know why. She watched as her best friend blew lightly on her tea, her eyes tracking Bria's bouncing steps past the picture window. And because her crush on Bria was fierce, Sully set her confusion aside as soon as Bria pushed into the café with a bright smile on her face and a basket full of treats in her hands.

Whatever was going on with Willie would just have to wait.

Bria was all Sully could think about for the moment.

WELCOME TO SEA PORT

TWO

Bria

It was possible that Bria had a bit of a reputation around town. Not for anything scandalous, unfortunately, mostly just for being a little bit reckless. She'd been a wild child — by Sea Port standards. Her mother, Evelyn Stone, used to call her "an absolute nightmare," but she said it with love and pride, so Bria had taken it as a compliment.

By Sea Port standards, of course.

In reality, Bria was a regular kid, just a little more rambunctious than the town was used to. Sure, there'd been a few years where she'd required bribes for good behavior, but what kid didn't? And sure, Bria and her roller skates might have inspired a town ordinance prohibiting anyone under the age of eighteen from roller-skating through traffic, but "traffic" in Sea Port was never more than a couple cars and maybe a couple horses, so Bria had only been ticketed a couple of times. Okay, and she had been pulled into the police station for tagging the high school with graffiti, but those charges were dropped, so did they even count? And actually, she did break into the senior high school to steal the valedictorian's medal, but it was just a prank and she returned it before graduation. So, even though Bria had a reputation, it wasn't nearly as bad as some people tried to make it out to be. And even if it had been, Bria's mother was fiercely protective of her only child, so they gossiped about her in private, the Sea Port way.

Anyone would want a mother like Evelyn. Bria was smart, artistic, funny, adventurous, and had a mind of her own — qualities Evelyn had painstakingly cultivated in her only child. Her mother's fierce and maybe at times over-bearing love was a blessing and a curse, but also because Bria had been born out of wedlock; something that still mattered in a place like Sea Port. No one besides Evelyn knew who her father was, not even Bria, so Evelyn tried her hardest to build an emotional fence around her daughter. She might not have had a father, but she had a mother who wouldn't think twice about cussing Pastor Leimert out if she had to.

Sea Port was always changing, but progress came slow in a town this small. Still, most Porties made their disapproval known about the circumstances of Bria's birth through cool silence to Evelyn's face for a few months and then just got over it, for the most part. And Evelyn took their judgment in stride because she felt she deserved it, but she always drew the line at anyone aiming anything that even sounded like a cross word at Bria. It was rare, but if anyone wondered where Bria got her attitude, they only had to look in her mother's direction.

Besides, Bria's rebellious childhood was just a phase. She graduated near the top of her class in high school and survived a few boring years in community college two towns over. She even got a job in Parkdale at an ice cream shop, although she'd had to borrow her mother's car to make it there and back. She loved Sea Port, but the town had been dying long before she was born, so leaving had been the only other option. Until it wasn't.

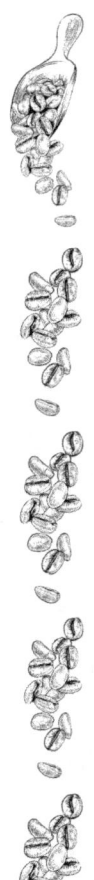

She'd been considering moving to Atlanta when Willie returned home. The town said goodbye to Skip Waltham in mournful hymns while his daughter launched her campaign for his job. Most people would've voted for Willie without a platform, but Bria had become a fan once she announced the Sea Port Relocation Initiative as a way to keep their beloved town from becoming a relic of a time long gone. Bria had been one of the first residents in Sea Port to support the idea besides the Walthams and happily told everyone she knew about the merits of the program. If they weren't convinced by logic, Bria wasn't above threats and blackmail. Thankfully, it never came to that. And as soon as Mary moved to Sea Port, Bria showed up to the old post office, résumé in hand, ready to get to work.

Evelyn cried big, fat, ugly tears when Bria got the job, which was a bit dramatic, but Bria let it slide because she'd wanted to cry herself.

Bria started at Confections with a plan to move from cashier to apprentice in record time and she'd done it. Technically, she was still Mary's apprentice, but they both knew she was ready for more responsibility. For the first time in her life, Bria didn't feel like Evelyn's wayward bastard daughter; she felt like herself. In Confections, Bria got to become her own person, and it felt amazing. *She* felt amazing, even if she worked from dawn to near dusk.

Usually Bria walked into Confections at the crack of dawn, beating Mary to the bakery more times than not — especially recently. She knew her tasks and she loved the quiet early mornings alone in the bakery, finding calm while prepping dough and making buttercream. She was usually halfway through a few starter doughs when Mary swanned into the bakery with a satisfied smile on her face and two coffees in hand. As far as Bria was concerned, this was the best job she could've hoped for. The fact that it was also in her hometown was royal icing on the cake.

Bria probably wouldn't have survived culinary school — she'd always been a bit funny about rigid structure — but learning under Mary had been a dream. Neither woman was professionally trained, and sometimes when they worked together, Bria felt less like Mary's apprentice and more like they were partners charting a path all their own. Every day at Confections was a new dough adventure.

Although, loving her job didn't solve all Bria's problems. It was easy to throw herself into work in a place like Sea Port because there wasn't much to do otherwise. She went in early because she was awake, so why not work, and she stayed after her shift technically ended because why not? Bria even covered for Charlie, their new cashier and general assistant, because she barely had a life outside of the bakery. Sometimes she stayed even if Mary didn't need her, experimenting with new recipes to pass the time before picking up a shift at La Bella Rosa whenever Sal needed help. There was so little to do in Sea Port that Bria's schedule was predictable as hell. Every other Thursday, she and Keith went to a double matinee feature at the art house theater in Parkdale, even if the movie looked terrible. And on Wednesdays, Bria broke up her long shift in the kitchen to make their weekly deliveries around town.

When Confections started supplying baked goods to local businesses, Bria had been the de facto delivery person because she was the only other employee. She'd split the deliveries with Charlie for a time, but as Bria's apprentice responsibilities increased, deliveries became Charlie's domain. This was a win-win situation since Charlie used her delivery route to glean the town's good gossip and bring it back to the bakery.

Busy as she was, though, Bria didn't give up her entire delivery route. Sea Port's best — and only — coffee shop required almost daily deliveries of Confections' most popular treats. Bria couldn't make all Sully's deliveries anymore, but she never missed Wednesday mornings, even if she was the only one who knew why.

She left Confections with a bright smile and a basket full of treats like she did every week. She walked the couple of blocks to the coffee shop with a slow, even gait. Sea Port was too damn small to be rushing anywhere, especially if she wanted to keep the town out of her business, but some days it was difficult to contain her excitement. Bria rounded the corner onto Freedom Way and ran a hand over her chin-length twists. She should've ducked into the bathroom to check her reflection before she left, but Charlie would've noticed, so she just hoped there wasn't a smear of flour on her face again. She started taking deep, calming breaths as she came onto Main Street. Halfway down the block, she spotted the café's sandwich board and smiled. Keith's lettering was getting better every week. She'd have to congratulate him on that later, though.

Wednesday mornings were all about Sully.

The coffee shop was packed as usual — by Sea Port standards. There were a couple of people in line to place their orders and most of the booths were occupied, but there couldn't have been more than twenty people in the entire building and she recognized every single one of them. Hell, some of the people in the coffee shop had known Bria since she had her baby teeth and she greeted them as she passed, but no matter which way she turned her head, she kept Sully squarely in her peripheral vision, drinking her in like a piping hot cup of her favorite white mocha latte.

Bria remembered the exact moment she realized she didn't just think Sully was cute but had a full-blown crush. Keith had just gotten his job as a trainee barista and had forced Bria to let him practice his skills on her when the café was empty. And because she was a good friend, she sipped dozens of his burnt espressos without complaint — well, without much complaint. That's what friends were for.

Her taste buds had been just on the edge of giving up the ghost when Sully walked into the café from the back room. Her hair was normally tied up in a bun at the back of her head, but that day, her dark brown curls were hanging down around her shoulders. She was wearing a black sports bra and baggy cargo pants slung low on her hips, with a bandana shoved into her back pocket. Bria had been mesmerized watching Sully haul boxes of drink stirrers and napkins to the self-serve station. Her stomach tightened, her mouth was dry, and lust was coursing through her veins like a sugar high. She'd been so caught up watching Sully, she forgot the cup in her hand was full of hot coffee and took a deep gulp without thinking.

It was peak irony that Keith's burned coffee burned the ever-loving shit out of her throat.

Bria started coughing uncontrollably; Keith started freaking out, pushing napkins into her hands to quiet her down, terrified her coughing fit would get him fired. Keith was panicking, Bria was gasping for breath, and Sully probably thought they were clowns.

"Are you alright?"

Bria's eyes were filled with tears but Sully's blurry image was beautiful.

Sully had a small stack of fresh napkins and pressed them into Bria's hands. She nodded in thanks and patted her eyes until her vision cleared, taking deep breaths until her tongue went mercifully numb. But relief just made room for hot embarrassment to eat away at the lust.

Keith tried to explain the situation — leaving out his burned espresso, of course — while Sully stood over Bria with a patient smile on her face.

"I'm alright," Bria finally croaked, even though every word hurt. "Just went down the wrong pipe."

"But it tasted good before that," Keith added hastily.

Bria glared at him while Sully laughed softly. "Let's get you some water," she said.

"I'll get it," Keith blurted out before scurrying away. Behind Sully's back, though, he put his hands up in prayer, a pleading look on his face. Bria got the message and swallowed carefully before turning back to Sully.

"It really was a good espresso shot," she lied.

Sully sat in Keith's empty seat and reached for Bria's

cup. Bria watched Sully lift the cup to her mouth with wide, shocked eyes. Sully smirked and took a small sip while Bria started mentally preparing to help Keith find a new job.

Sully watched Bria while she sipped, swallowed, and then set the cup back on the table. She rested her hands in her lap and shook her head. "It was not a good espresso shot," she said with a soft smile, "but I know he'll get better."

Bria had a defense on the tip of her tongue, but Sully was looking in the eyes with a calm but somehow also intense gaze. She had known Sully in passing for years, but that moment pushed Bria's mostly innocent admiration into serious crush territory.

SULLY

"What have ya got for me today?" Sully asked as soon as Bria stepped behind the counter. She tried to sound casual, but she always seemed to stumble over her words when Bria was around.

"The usual," Bria smiled. "Cinnamon rolls, some lemon teacakes, assorted muffins, scones."

Sully opened her mouth, but Lorraine leaned over the counter, invading their space. "Blueberry muffins?"

Bria laughed softly and opened her basket. "Yeah, a few

blueberry muffins," she said, carefully poking through the basket in her hands.

"Two, please," Lorraine requested, holding out her hand.

Bria looked to Sully, who rolled her eyes and nodded. "She prepaid. Here, let me take the basket. You can open the display case."

Bria handed the basket over. Their fingers brushed, just for a second, and Sully's stomach clenched.

"Muffins," Lorraine whispered impatiently.

Sully glared at her before reaching into the basket. "You want a bag?"

"Nah. We both know I'm gonna eat one of these on the way to work."

"You work across the street," Bria said as Sully put the individually wrapped muffins into Lorraine's hands.

"Don't judge me," Lorraine said. "Me and my sweet tooth keep you working for Mary instead of... Actually, what would you do if Confections never opened?"

Bria bounced back up. "I try not to imagine that dark timeline. We'll make sure to put a couple more blueberry muffins in the next order."

Lorraine beamed. "Thank you kindly," she said, before rushing from the café.

"Did you see 'em?" Bria asked excitedly.

"See what?"

A mischievous grin spread over Bria's mouth, exposing the suggestion of a dimple on her left cheek. Sully always paid close attention to that dimple as it deepened and sank into Bria's soft skin. She desperately wanted to explore that dimple with her lips.

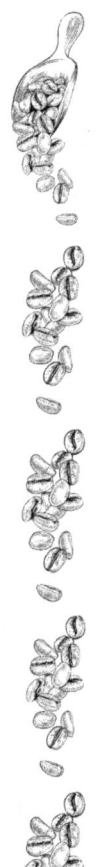

Bria reached into the basket and pulled the top tray from the case, minus two muffins. She lifted her eyebrows at Sully and inclined her head toward the basket.

Sully was too busy watching her, however, that it took a few seconds for her to follow Bria's direction, but when she did, she gasped. "Mary made bagels?"

Bria pursed her lips. "*I* made bagels," she said, rolling her eyes.

"You...did?"

Bria's smile returned. "You said you wished you could get fresh bagels in Sea Port."

"I did," Sully agreed, even though she only had a vague memory of that conversation. If it even was a conversation.

"And I remembered," Bria said cheerily. "I've been working on a recipe for a bit. This is the first batch I think is good enough to sell, but I'm totally open to feedback, um... from anyone. Just, uh, let me know how they do. And if you try one, um...you know, let me know what you think."

Her entire coffee shop disappeared for a minute. Sure, she knew the building was packed and loud, but for a few moments Sully couldn't see or hear anything or anyone else. If it wasn't Bria, her brain refused to acknowledge it.

It didn't help that they were standing close enough to touch. If she lifted her hand, her fingers could brush the end of one of Bria's twists. If she took a half-step forward, some part of their bodies would surely kiss.

And if Sully weren't such a coward, she would've done either of those things, but she didn't. Instead, Sully reached inside the basket and marveled at the soft bagel Bria had made. She tried to convince herself that they were just bagels — just balls of dough, baked or fried or boiled, she didn't even know — that would expand her successful relationship with Confections. These bagels were small, insignificant things in the grand scheme of her small business; there was really no need to swoon over them or the woman who'd made them.

She tried — she really did — and failed. Bria had learned how to make bagels because Sully wanted them, and that didn't feel small or insignificant at all.

"I..." Sully's voice cracked, pulling the sounds of the coffee shop back into her brain. She looked away and took a shallow breath before turning back. "Um, thanks. Thank you. I'll definitely try one and report back."

Bria beamed at Sully before grabbing the basket and turning back to the display case, stocking it quickly and efficiently.

Sully watched her for a few seconds before clearing her throat. "Do you need any help?" she asked, unsure what to do with herself now that their usual chat seemed to be over.

"No, thanks," Bria said, smiling up at her. "But if you've got the old trays and the coffee for me to take back, that'd be great."

"Oh, yeah. Of course," Sully said quickly, remembering herself finally.

In exchange for making all the café's baked goods, Sully roasted and ground a special blend of coffee especially for the bakery. They swapped their wares a couple times a week and split the profit evenly. Sometimes Sully thought she was getting far more than she gave, but then she remembered that Mary was on the road to Sea Port domination and Sully's was just her first stop.

She usually set the trays and coffee aside but she'd

forgotten to gather everything earlier. Thankfully, she had brewed the coffee; she just needed to fill up the jugs for transport. Once that was done, she looked for the empty trays from her last order, realizing eventually that she'd left them in the back room. She instantly blamed her excitement at Bria's arrival for being so out of sorts, but then remembered that actually, it was Willie who'd set her off track.

At that thought, she cast a quick glance toward the front window and found her best friend sitting on the edge of a stool, her eyes trained directly on Bria. Now she knew for sure something was up with Willie, but that was a matter for a later date.

Sully ducked into the back room and grabbed the trays. By the time she returned, the display case was full and Bria had set aside the extra items for Sully to store in the back fridge. Sully handed over the old trays and Bria packed them into her case while Sully grabbed the coffee, placing the cartons carefully on top of the trays.

"You sure that's not too heavy?"

Bria laughed. "Nah. You'd be surprised how much upper body strength you need to knead enough dough to keep our cases full. I'm stronger than ever these days."

Sully's eyes moved to Bria's bicep but she dragged her gaze away before they started to roam. "Makes sense," she croaked.

"Alright, that's it. Um...it was nice seeing you." Bria smiled.

Sully felt like the sun was shining down on her. "Yeah, it was...it was really nice to see you too."

They smiled at one another for a bit longer before Bria turned and made her way toward the door. Sully watched her hungrily as she waved to a few customers on her way out. She pulled the front door open and then she was gone, but Sully refused to look away. She watched Bria through the shop's front window until her eyes landed on the back of Willie's head.

Willie was watching Bria leave as well.

WELCOME TO SEA PORT

THREE

Bria

The walk from Confections to Sully's always took Bria three minutes, but the walk from Sully's back to the bakery took five minutes at least. Her gait was slower, her heart was racing, and Bria used every step to pore over her conversation with Sully in deliciously excruciating detail. Usually, Bria used this walk to lightly castigate herself for her one-sided crush, but some days — like today — she was sure there was something there. It wasn't just their quick little chat or the way Sully watched her while she worked, it was the way she *looked* at her — that couldn't be nothing. It wasn't nothing on Bria's end, that was for sure.

As much as Bria had tried to rein her feelings in, she knew the mask slipped when Sully smiled at the tray of bagels. Bagels Bria went into work an hour early to make just for her. She worked hard every day at Confections, but watching a blush spread over Sully's cheeks validated all the time she spent reading bagel recipes, every test batch she'd ruined. And she did it all for Sully. To Bria, it wouldn't matter who ate and loved her bagels as long as Sully did. It had been a gamble to focus so much time learning how to make bagels since Mary thought the market for them in Sea Port would be small, but Sully liked them. Sully wanted them. And Bria had made it happen.

"What you smilin' 'bout, girl?" Mr. Johnson asked, stopping Bria in her tracks. He was standing in the street, one hand on the door handle of his work truck, the other clutching a Confections box. He was eyeing her with suspicion like he had ever since she allegedly graffitied Mr. Jones's barn. Not even his barn! Mr. Johnson just loved to hold a grudge.

She had a few smart answers to his question, but she didn't need her slick tongue getting back to her mother. Not when she'd been doing so well as a functioning member of Sea Port society.

"Hey, Mr. Johnson. How are you doing today?" He glared at her, but she kept going. "I hope you like this week's biscuits. I made 'em." He hated when she ignored his ire, but he really hated being reminded that she had more than a little to do with his buttermilk biscuit addiction.

He sucked his teeth loudly and pulled the truck door open.

Bria continued walking back to work but made sure to wave disrespectfully at Mr. Johnson through the passenger window as she passed. She already couldn't stand the man, but now that he'd robbed her of a few moments of thinking about Sully, she was more annoyed with him than normal.

All too soon, Bria was reaching for the front door to Confections when someone inside pulled it open for her. Santos's stern but kind face greeted her.

"What's shakin', bacon?" she called.

His smile fell away and he shook his head while moving aside to let her enter. "You've gotta stop calling me a pig, Bria. We're friends?"

Bria smiled and walked past him across the small dining room and through the swinging half-door separating the storefront from the serving area. "I know, that's why I call you 'bacon.' I love bacon."

She came up with a new excuse every time he called her out — it was becoming their thing. She called him a pork product, he pretended to be annoyed about it, rinse and repeat.

"Bullshit," he breathed, trying to stop himself from laughing. Santos rolled his eyes but his smile was back, kind and indulgent. Bria was an only child, so when Santos and Knox started treating Bria like their annoying little sister, she ate that shit up. She'd always wanted siblings and Mary, Knox, and Santos were close enough.

"Where are you coming from?" Santos asked, closing the shop's door.

"Sully's. Weekly delivery." She set the basket in her hand on the counter and pulled out the jugs of coffee.

"Ah," Santos said.

Bria looked up from the basket, but Santos turned his head to scan the empty sidewalk in front of the bakery. Her face was warm again, and not from her walk. She was just about to ask him what the hell that "ah" meant when Mary pushed the swinging kitchen door open, followed closely by Knox.

"We need to book the time off," Knox said in a voice

softened by so much love. He was hovering close at Mary's back, almost stepping on her heels.

"Soon," Mary sighed weakly. Her eyes darted around the shop and when they settled on Bria, she almost looked relieved, which was odd. "Bria, you're back! How did it go?" she asked, changing the subject. Also odd.

Knox pursed his lips before locking eyes with Santos across the room. The look of exasperation was the third in a trifecta of "what the fuck is going on?" and Bria didn't like it.

"It went fine," said Bria. She could tell Mary needed a save, and because Mary was her boss and her friend, she threw her a lifeline. "I dropped off the first test batch of bagels today. I'll be ready to tweak the recipe when we get feedback."

Mary squinted at her, probably wondering what the hell she was talking about, but she hid it well and took the opening Bria offered.

Nodding gravely, Mary spun around and placed her hands on Knox's chest. She leaned into his body. "Hear that, babe? We've got important baking business to handle. We can talk about this later, okay?"

Santos chuckled, and when Bria glanced at him, he'd ducked his shaking head to hide his laughter.

Knox wrapped his arms around Mary's waist and pulled her into him. "It's only 'cause I love you that I'm gonna let you brush me off like this. Next time, do better."

"I'll try," Mary said in a low voice that was none of Bria's business. She turned around just as Knox bent forward to press his lips to Mary's. Bria grabbed the trays from the basket and walked them to the sink just behind them, averting her eyes and closing her ears to whatever he was whispering to her. Sometimes Bria got sad watching everyone else be so in love while she was grasping onto literal crumbs with Sully, but there was always more work to do, thankfully. While Knox and Mary practically made out in the middle of the shop and Santos watched them with a hungry look on his face, Bria stowed the delivery basket, washed her hands, and checked the display case to see what needed replenishing.

She was shifting the chocolate cream donuts to make room for a fresh batch when Mary and Knox finally let one another go only to walk into the storefront. He kept his hands on Mary's hips as she lifted onto the balls of her feet, offering her mouth to Santos. Thankfully, the acoustics were bad and Bria couldn't hear whatever Mary whispered to him. Unfortunately, nothing could make her unhear Knox's dirty laughter.

Bria was refilling the donut case when Santos and Knox finally let Mary go and turned toward the door.

"Hey, kid," Knox said, stepping close to the other side of the display case.

Bria rolled her eyes. "I'm not a kid."

He laughed softly. "Then lie better next time."

"It wasn't a lie. We really do have bagels to make."

"Sure," he laughed. Santos chuckled again and pulled the door open. Knox pushed his sunglasses onto his face and shot her one of those annoyingly handsome smiles. "Sure you do, kid."

Bria flipped him off as he left.

Mary shut the door behind them before rounding on Bria. "What bagels?"

"Huh?" Bria's mouth fell open. She abandoned the donut restock and turned toward the kitchen. Knox was right; she needed to improve her lying skills.

"What bagels, Bria?" Mary asked, following her into the kitchen.

"I know neither of us went to culinary school, but we both know what bagels are," Bria called over her shoulder. She moved to the clipboard nailed to the wall next to the fridge to check their dough schedule for the afternoon — anything to avoid making eye contact with Mary as she came laughing into the kitchen.

Bria moved to the prep sink to wash her hands. Mary walked across the room, crossed her arms, and leaned back against the wall. Bria tried her best to ignore Mary.

"You get snarky when you're nervous, so this is gonna be good. Now I know I'm giving you more responsibilities, but when did Confections start making bagels?"

Bria soaped her hands like she was a surgeon preparing for the operating room. "I talked to you about bagels."

"And I told you I didn't think they'd work."

Bria rinsed her hands while grasping for what to say next. She ripped two paper towels from the dispenser and dried her hands thoroughly, mentally castigating herself for not preparing a good lie for this inevitable conversation *before* she delivered the first batch to Sully's. She'd just been so excited.

She threw the paper towels in the trash and just started talking. "You said we needed some more exclusive products for Sully's."

Mary's face was full of amusement. "I was thinking

along the lines of new cookie recipes or more lollipops," she replied.

"We already have enough cookies," Bria said.

"Blasphemy!" Mary gasped.

"Coffee shops have bagels!" Bria laughed as she moved across the kitchen to the refrigerator. She wrenched it open to see if they needed more buttercream. She could feel Mary's gaze on her back, but it took a few seconds for Bria to register the silence. She counted the containers of frosting twice before she gave up, closed the fridge, and turned around. Mary was still leaning against the wall, arms crossed and a small, knowing smile on her face. Now she knew what Santos's "ah" had meant.

"How long have you known?"

The smile on Mary's face wasn't one Bria had seen before. It wasn't the bright "Welcome to Confections" smile she used when greeting customers, or the slightly dirty "Come taste my muffins" smile for when she was flirting with Santos or Knox or Lorraine or Sully or Bria or... Well, half the town, now that Bria thought of it. The woman really was shameless. But this also wasn't the "Calgon, take me away" well-fucked smile plastered on her face each morning either. This smile was devious.

"Known what?" Mary asked innocently. "Oh! You mean how long have I known about your adorable little crush on Sully?"

"It's not a crush," Bria replied quickly, sweat collecting at her hairline.

"Infatuation?" Mary offered, lifting her eyebrows earnestly.

Bria didn't know how to answer that, so she licked her

lips and wondered if Mary remembered to feed their sour-dough starter.

Mary pushed off the wall, dropped her arms, and started walking toward her. "I've known about that little situation for almost a year. Were you trying to hide it?"

Bria shook her head. "It hasn't been that long," she said, feeling frantic and exposed.

"Oh, babe," Mary sighed. "If you say so."

"I need to sit down," Bria muttered. She walked across the room and fell into the chair at the small desk Mary kept in the kitchen for baking admin.

Mary was undeterred by her distress. "So, are the bagels your lesbian version of flowers? Did you ask her out? Did she say yes?" Each question seemed to build up in Mary's system and she was practically bouncing in excitement.

Bria's mouth opened and closed. And then opened and closed again. "Am I really that obvious?"

Mary snorted a laugh. "Oh, yes. Very obvious. We've been talking about that adorable stutter thing you do when she stops by."

"I don't stutter," Bria said, feeling as if maybe Knox was right to call her a kid.

"Oh, yes, you do, but only with her. You also do this super cute thing where you just keep wiping your hands down the front of your apron—" Mary demonstrated once before dissolving into giggles.

Bria wanted to defend herself, but she could literally picture herself doing just what Mary described. "I... Why didn't Keith tell me I was this obvious?" she moaned, dropping her head to her hands, but only for a second. "And how did *you* of all people notice?"

"Hey!" Mary said, throwing her arms out in protest. "What's that supposed to mean?"

Bria pursed her lips and tilted her head in disbelief. "That means you've had your hands full with the cop and the fire chief for almost as long as I've known you."

"Stop calling them that. *'The baker, the cop, and the fire chief',*" Mary mimicked in a childish chant. "Why do you all call us that? You know our names!"

Bria stared at her for a few seconds. "'Cause it's funny," she answered simply. "And you three are always very busy, together and apart. How do you have time to notice anything besides those two and the bakery?"

Mary leveled Bria with a look that was less mirthful and more loving older sister. "I might be...busy." She stopped here and smiled to herself.

"See?" Bria whispered.

Mary straightened her face and glared down at her. "But you're our friend, we love you. Also we're nosy as fuck."

Mary's words and her sincerity pulled all the indignant fight out of Bria. Her face was hot from emotion and she tried her hardest not to cry happy tears. More only-child feelings bubbling to the surface.

Mary walked toward her and placed a hand on Bria's shoulder. "Between Lorraine and Jonah and you and Sully, we've had a lot of gossip to share at night. It's so much better when it's not about you."

Bria shook her head softly. "There's no me and Sully."

"Well, there sure won't be if you don't say anything to her." Mary paused, chewed her bottom lip, and then continued, "Or if she doesn't say anything to you."

Bria gave herself two full seconds to feel all the pathetic

hope she normally denied herself before shoving it down in her gut. "She doesn't... You don't think—" She couldn't bring herself to finish either of those sentences.

Mary sucked her teeth and patted Bria's shoulder before turning away. "Wow, you two are hopeless."

Bria watched Mary move to the sink and start washing her hands before something pinged in her brain. "Hold on. What time off?"

WELCOME TO SEA PORT

FOUR

Sully

It was a three-minute walk — two minutes if she walked quickly — but Sully could make the walk last as long as five minutes if she stopped by the Sunnyside to say hey and she let Mr. Johnson talk to her about where she sourced her milk and why wasn't it from his dairy farm. The trick was to never walk fast enough to arouse the attention of anyone over the age of fifty-seven, which was a lot harder to do in a town as small and nosy as Sea Port. And it was especially hard on an evening like tonight, where adrenaline had Sully's pulse pounding a hundred-fifty miles an hour.

She'd walked this path from her coffee shop to Confections countless times. Even their nosy neighbors wouldn't have been surprised to see Sully stopping by the bakery, and not just because they were Transplants. Sully and Mary had a strong business relationship and this was business.

Mostly.

Bria had gone out of her way to make bagels just for

Sully's and she'd asked for feedback. Sully had thoughts, lots of them. So, instead of going home after the café closed, she was walking to Confections to give Bria what she asked for. Feedback.

Just feedback.

Probably.

She'd spent the entire closing shift going over how the next few moments would unfold. When she got to Confections, she'd make sure Bria was there. If she wasn't, Sully would order a cinnamon roll to go. If Bria was there, Sully would wait for her to be free and then pull her aside. She'd say hi, like a normal person. They'd chat about their days or the weather for a little bit, like normal people. And then, finally, she'd tell Bria that her bagels were literally the best she'd ever had...but like a normal person. She wouldn't mention that she'd taken two bagels home on her break just so she could toast them and smear an ungodly amount of cream cheese onto the slices. She'd enjoyed them in a peace exacerbated by knowing that Bria had made them with her own hands because Sully had asked.

For a second, Sully had imagined that Bria would be gracious at her compliments, but that wasn't the Bria she knew and had become obsessed with. The Bria she knew would interrogate her like she always did when workshopping a recipe. So while Sully was mopping the floor and Keith broke down boxes in the storeroom, she came up with answers for questions Bria would surely ask about texture, taste, and how they'd toasted. She had answers at the ready, and if it went really well, Sully had plans to buy an orange scone to stress-eat on the walk home. Like a normal person who was too terrified to tell Bria how much she liked her.

"Yep," Sully mumbled, stepping onto the curb in front of Confections. "Super normal and pathetic."

Sully had to squeeze into the shop with the rest of the late-evening Confections crowd. She couldn't find a line, so she found a space behind Tom Miles, who owned the hardware store next door. By the looks of his overalls and crisp black work shirt, Sully thought Tom had closed his shop and come straight to Confections, so at least she wasn't alone in her post-work pit stop.

She scanned the bakery looking for Bria. Charlie was standing behind the mostly empty display case with tongs raised in the air and a bored look on her face while waiting for Tom to pick out which cookies he wanted for his lodge meeting later tonight. Ashton Moore, one of the few teenagers in town and Charlie's little brother, was waiting with a five-dollar bill clutched in his hand and his eyes laser-focused on the very last pecan roll in the display case. Ann Lester was waiting by the cash register, and Mary was at the prep table, carefully boxing up a cake. But Bria was nowhere to be found.

"Welcome to Confections, give us a minute," Mary called tiredly, never taking her attention from the cake.

Sully nodded and shifted her gaze to the door that led to the kitchen. She didn't know Bria's schedule and disappointment bubbled in her chest that she'd missed her. She thought about leaving, but there were two cinnamon rolls in the display case and her feelings wouldn't eat themselves, so she moved to one of the tables in the small sitting area and resigned herself to wait.

Confections closed in the next hour or so — or whenever their cases were empty, whichever came first. Sully

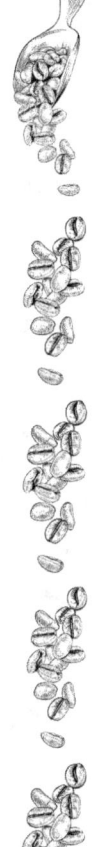

didn't mind waiting. She never had much to do in the evening anyway. No matter when she left the coffee shop, she usually walked home — with maybe a pit stop at the grocery store on her way — and showered. Sometimes, she waited for Willie to get home so they could catch up about their days over a late dinner.

Tom finally started carefully selecting cookies. "Lemme get those two teacakes in the front. No, those," he said.

Charlie sighed loudly. "They're from the same batch."

"Those two in the front," Tom repeated.

Ashton sucked his teeth.

"Alright, here we are, Mrs. Lester. German chocolate with bourbon chocolate filling."

"Bourbon chocolate?" Tom asked. "That come in a cookie?"

Mary laughed. "No, this was a special order. It's Ann and Martin's fortieth anniversary." She had a smile on her face as if she was getting an invitation to the party — if there was a party. But then Mary's face froze and her eyes lifted to the ceiling in thought. "Although I guess I could make it into a donut."

Mrs. Lester laughed. "If you do that, let me know. It's easier and cheaper to buy some donuts than lingerie."

Sully's eyes widened and Mary's gaze shifted to hers. They both tried not to smile in shock.

"Well, I'll keep that in mind," Mary said. "Have fun tonight!"

Mrs. Lester picked up her cake with a smile. "Believe me, we will."

Sully almost broke at that but covered her smile with a fist.

When she was gone, Ashton turned to his sister. "What's lingerie?"

Charlie's eyes widened but Mary intervened. "Ashton, I'll give you the pecan roll for free if you forget everything you just heard."

He swung back in Mary's direction. "Deal."

Mary wrapped his treat and handed it over with a smile.

"You can sit on the bench outside and wait for me. I'll be done soon," Charlie called to her brother while grabbing the last of Tom's cookies.

Ashton nodded on his way out the door, but most of his attention was on his pastry. Sully watched him settle on the bench outside and open the box with his treat, carefully picking some of the pecan pieces from the frosting. He was going to savor every inch of that pecan roll. She envied Ashton's childlike pleasure; it looked far more exciting than Sully's inner turmoil.

Mary cleared her throat to get Sully's attention. "How can I help you, Ms. Sullivan?"

Sully pursed her lips. "The only people who call me that are debt collectors," she said.

Mary smiled and rested her elbows on the counter next to the register. "What's up, Sully? You here for business or pleasure?"

Sully's mouth went dry. "Pleasure?" she croaked out.

Mary's face lit up. "We gotta few of those scones you like left. Buy one, get one half-off, just for you." She winked.

Sully let out a soft laugh and wiped at the sweat on her forehead with the heel of her right hand. "Maybe," she said, even though she knew those scones were going home with her. "But I guess I'm here for business...actually."

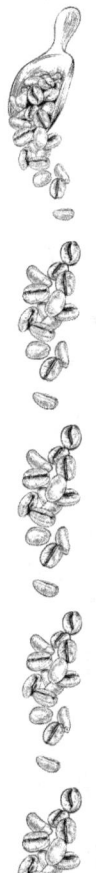

Mary's face fell. "Oh. What's up?"

Charlie bumped Mary out of the way with her hip so she could ring up Tom's cookies.

Sully stood from her chair and smoothed her hands down the front of her t-shirt.

"Um... Bria brought some bagels to the café today."

"Y'all making bagels now?" Tom asked, the box of cookies in his hand. His gaze moved between Mary's face and the display case.

"Wait, are we?" Charlie asked.

Mary's attention was focused on Sully, a small smile on her mouth. "Not yet. It's Bria's project." She turned to Tom. "But we'll let you know when we start rolling them out."

"Alright now," Tom said, nodding his head at each woman before walking from the store.

"Um..." Sully swallowed the lump in her throat. "She told me if I had any feedback, she wanted to hear it, and I—"

Mary held her hand up and turned her body halfway toward the back of the shop. "Bria, can you come out here, please?"

Sully's heart actually stopped beating for a moment. All three women stood there in silence, waiting, until Bria pushed into the storefront a few seconds later in a flour-covered apron and her twists pulled into a bun on top of her head. Sully's gaze tracked her steps across the storefront.

Bria was distracted and looking down at a recipe card in her hands. "What?"

"Look who's here," Mary said.

Bria looked up with bunched eyebrows, but then her mouth fell open and she stopped walking halfway between the kitchen and the cash register. "Hi," she breathed.

"Hi." It had been a long day at work. That was Sully's excuse for why she couldn't stop smiling as soon as she locked eyes with Bria. She felt like a teenager come to pick her girlfriend up for a date and she hated how happy the feeling made her because it wasn't true.

"Sully stopped by to give you feedback on your contraband bagels," Mary trilled.

"Contraband?" Sully asked.

Bria cut her eyes quickly in Mary's direction before refocusing on Sully. "Did you like them?" Her soft voice pulled at Sully's heartstrings — she sounded nervous and hopeful at the same time, just like Sully felt.

"I loved them," she breathed, all the reverence she felt for Bria softening the edges of her own words. Sully felt exposed by the way Bria was staring back at her — as if she was really seeing her for the first time — and it felt far too good to be true.

"Well, then," Mary giggled. "Come on, Charlie. There's some baking dough icing stuff I want to show you. In the kitchen. In the back. Not out here."

Bria and Sully looked away from one another. Sully wiped at her damp forehead and breathed deep.

"No, thanks, boss," Charlie said brightly. "I'm just here to sell the sugary crack and eat the sugary crack, don't need to make it too. I'll stay here just in case someone else drops in. Besides, I've been waiting all season for this development."

"Girl, if you don't—" Mary huffed. "Fine, you can go home."

"Oop, ain't gotta tell me twice!' Charlie said excitedly.

She stooped behind the register and popped back up with her purse. "Y'all have a good night."

Mary shook her head and headed toward the kitchen. "You two have fun."

"Go away," Bria sighed.

Mary disappeared into the kitchen, leaving Sully alone with Bria for the first time ever.

She felt like her heart was about to burst out of her chest, but in a good way.

WELCOME TO SEA PORT

FIVE

Bria

Ontrary to what her mom said, Bria wasn't much of a dreamer. Even when she'd had braces and been fantasizing about leaving Sea Port, she was never planning to leave for good. E*very* teenager in Sea Port dreamed about leaving — it was basically a rite of passage — because Sea Port was too damn small to do anything besides leave. But in the past few years, her tiny little hometown had become surprisingly fertile ground for Bria's new dreams, especially if they had to do with Sully.

Most days, she rushed to bed just so she could dream about her. In her imagination, the bakery was empty and it was always raining. Why rain? Because Bria thought it was romantic. She'd be closing the shop alone when Sully showed up in the same kind of cargo pants she always wore around the café, but a tight tank top instead of the baggy band tees she preferred. And no bra. That last part was very important whenever she was face down in her bed, a hand shoved into her panties, using her pillow to muffle her moans. It was the ultimate fantasy — there were no health codes so they could have sex on every surface in the bakery and she didn't have to clean and disinfect the shop after. It was heavenly.

This wasn't like her dream at all, but Sully liked her bagels, so that was cool too.

"Sorry about that. Mary and Charlie are nosy as hell," Bria said, sounding breathless and feeling lightheaded. She was trying her best not to fidget, but after months of feeling near desperate for Sully's attention, now that she had it, she didn't know what to do with it.

"I work with your best friend," Sully smirked. "I've never met anyone nosier than him."

Bria smiled so wide her cheeks hurt. "I've been telling him that our whole life," she laughed, taking a step forward.

Sully stepped forward as well, and they met — as they often had over the past few months — with only a small counter between them.

"So you...you really liked my bagels?" Bria asked.

Sully's face lit up. "I did. I loved them. I took a couple home for lunch."

The words fell out of her mouth in an excited rush. Bria had been watching Sully with a secret delight for almost a year. She'd never seen her this animated before. It was glorious.

It might have been a little egotistical, but listening to Sully talk about enjoying her bagels in detail made Bria's small but mighty crush grow like a garden of wildflowers after a heavy rain.

"After I was done eating, I realized I should have tried

one without toasting them, so I'm going to do that tomorrow. I want to give them a firm test drive, you know?"

"Um, how many did you...sell?" Bria asked.

Sully's face froze and her head tilted slightly to the left in consideration. Bria was happy her hands were hidden under the counter because the urge to touch Sully — any part of her — was so intense, she was balling her apron into her fists just out of view.

"Technically..." Sully started as an adorable blush spread across her light brown cheeks. "None."

Bria's smile fell. "None?"

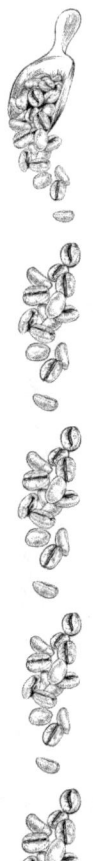

Sully shook her head. "It's not what you think," she said quickly. "It's just... You know, you made them for me, so I thought—" Sully stopped here and ran her hands over her hair even though not a single curl was out of place.

Bria's mouth fell open. "You ate them all?"

"Not yet," Sully replied, shaking her head a few more times before her expression shifted. "But I'm going to."

There was usually a tiny kaleidoscope of butterflies in Bria's stomach having a little party whenever she saw Sully, but they went absolutely apeshit at the conviction in her voice. "God, you're so—" Bria started to say but then clamped her lips shut.

Sully's eyebrows bunched together. "So...what?"

Bria let go of her apron and smoothed her hands over the wrinkled material. She licked her lips nervously. Sully's eyes were focused on Bria's mouth and somehow, that gave her the courage to finish that sentence. "Amazing. I think you're so fucking amazing."

If she'd thought admitting her feelings would give her

some relief, she was wrong. Somehow, telling Sully how she felt only made Bria feel so much more.

"I think you're beautiful," Sully blurted out, her cheeks flushed red. She sighed gently and shook her head. "I've wanted to tell you that for over a year, but I'm such a coward. And I didn't even know if you were gay—"

"I'm gay!" Bria blurted out excitedly. "Very, very gay. Big lesbian." It took a second for her brain to catch up with her mouth. "I can't believe I just said that."

Sully's laugh finally broke through. Her laughter was like music to Bria's ears and took away some of the sting. Bria thought she heard Mary giggling from the kitchen, but she forgot about her when Sully put her palms on the counter and leaned forward.

"Very, *very* gay, huh?" Sully's voice was deeper, silkier, and it washed over her like water, electrifying each hair on her arms and the back of her neck before running down her spine. Her hands were shaking as she placed them on the counter, close enough for their fingers to touch if either woman had the courage.

"Very," Bria sighed, leaning forward and letting the faintly bitter scent of coffee beans on Sully's skin fill her nostrils. That smell had been haunting her for months and it stoked a flame inside her chest. Bria wanted Sully something fierce — to touch her, smell her, taste her. And maybe Sully could read her mind or she was thinking the same things because they ran their tongues over their lips at the same time.

"Have dinner with me tonight?" Bria breathed.

"I was just about to ask you that," Sully laughed. Their fingers finally touched on the counter and slid together.

Bria felt like she was floating. "You can ask me next time," she replied.

Sully looked almost as happy as Bria felt and it emboldened her to do something she'd been wanting for months. She started to lean forward, her stomach rumbling in hunger as her gaze focused on Sully's mouth, but then the bell over the front door chimed, ruining the moment. They jumped away from one another and Bria's eyes shifted to glare at the intruder.

Or customer. Whatever.

"Come on!" Mary yelled from the kitchen.

"Well, what do we have here?" Old Ms. Kemp said, sauntering inside the bakery. Bria could tell from the smile on her face that they were going to be at the top of the WAKC agenda next.

She sighed in frustration but put a professional smile on her face and glanced at the clock above the door. "Welcome to Confections, Ms. Kemp. We close in half an hour. What can I get for you today?"

Old Ms. Kemp's gaze flitted from Bria to Sully and back. Sully shoved her hands into her back pockets in her peripheral vision and Bria's stomach dropped. They'd been so close to the best thing to happen to Bria since Confections opened.

"Do you have any more pound cake slices?" Ms. Kemp asked.

Bria had to swallow her rage before she could speak, gesturing with her right hand. "Middle display case," she said in a short voice. Ms. Kemp nodded before moving away.

Sully was already stepping toward the door. "See you

tonight?" Bria asked excitedly, refusing to let this moment slip through her fingers.

Sully stopped mid-step. "Absolutely. I can come back once you're done with closing."

"Actually, let's meet at La Bella Rosa."

Mary burst through into the storefront. "We'll be quick," she called. "Twenty-five minutes after closing, tops."

"Mary!" Bria hissed.

"I shouldn't have sent Charlie home," Mary sighed sadly.

"Okay," Sully laughed. When Bria turned toward her, Sully waited until their eyes locked once more. "I can't wait."

Bria swooned.

And her nipples got hard.

"Me neither," she sighed in return.

WELCOME TO SEA PORT

SIX

Sully

S ully had never run home, showered, and changed so
fast. She pulled on her dressiest pair of linen pants, a
tank top, and an open button-up shirt. She checked
her reflection in the mirror, sprayed some cologne on her
neck, and rushed out the front door.

She locked her door and turned toward Willie's side of
their duplex.

Living next door to each other was her best friend's idea;
Sully had just been happy for a place to lay her head. They
went from an expensive high-rise apartment in Chicago to
paying less than a third of their former rent with even more
space. At first, it had been like living in dorms again, barging
into one another's homes to watch terrible reality dating
shows together, but as their responsibilities increased, they
had less and less time to spend with one another. Sully
couldn't even count how many times she'd stood in front of
Willie's door waiting for her friend to answer and been
disappointed, so she called Willie's office instead.

"What?" Willie sighed on the other end of the line.

"If that's how you're answering the phone, it might be time to quit," Sully said.

"Believe me, I've thought about it. What's up?"

"Nothing, just seeing where you were and what you were doing."

"At work. Working. What are you doing?"

"Nothing. About to eat dinner," Sully said casually even as her stomach flipped in excitement.

"My stomach just growled. What are you making?"

Sully's eyes widened in panic. "Um, I don't know. I think I have a few eggs, a quarter of a bell pepper. Leftover chili from—"

"Never mind, never mind," Willie said. She absolutely hated Sully's leftover concoctions. "I'll order a burger from the Sunnyside."

"Don't work too hard," Sully laughed, bouncing down their front steps.

"Don't die of food poisoning," Willie shot back, and they hung up without saying goodbye.

Sully had been waiting for this night for months. So. Many. Long. Months. She hadn't been on a date since at least a year before she moved to Sea Port, when she'd been a workaholic who wouldn't have recognized work-life balance if it smacked her in the face. All she remembered about that date was that it lasted an entire weekend until the girl's wife came home. She was fine but more drama than she was worth, so Sully threw herself into work instead. And then she'd given up on dating altogether when she moved to Sea Port. She'd figured the town would be full of nothing but old straight people but was happy to find out that she was only partially correct. There were queer couples in town, but they'd been together for almost as long as Sully had been alive, so she was still dateless as hell.

Until Bria. Until tonight.

She arrived at La Bella Rosa a full five minutes early and waited outside the restaurant. Unlike the little downtown corridor, Sea Port's only Italian restaurant was set in a small alcove that had seen better days. There used to be other buildings out here, other businesses Porties needed but had disappeared one by one. Now there was just the restaurant, a fabric store and craft shop Sully had never once even stepped inside, and a perfect view of the new library, but that would change soon enough if Willie had anything to say about it.

Sully power walked across town and tried to settle her breathing before Bria showed up, but a couple minutes after she arrived, a heavy metal door half a block down from the restaurant groaned open and Bria stepped onto the sidewalk.

Bria had a work uniform just as much as Sully — dark leggings and long t-shirts, usually covered in flour smudges — but when she stepped onto the sidewalk, she was wearing a short black halter dress. Sully had never seen so much of Bria's skin and she didn't know where to look. When she managed to lift her eyes to Bria's face, she couldn't help but smile.

Bria looked adorably nervous, twisting her fingers together as she walked toward Sully. "You're early," she breathed.

Sully's eyes skimmed down Bria's body again before she checked her watch. "So are you. How fast did you and Mary clean the bakery?"

Bria's smile was accentuated by a sheen of clear lip gloss. "She let me go early. She didn't want me to be late."

"I'll remember to thank her," Sully whispered.

Bria rolled her eyes. "Don't. If you give her an inch, she'll take a mile and be all in our business forever."

Sully ducked her head to laugh. "The whole town will be in our business no matter what," she chuckled, but then her smile faltered. "You okay with that?"

Bria laughed harder. "This is all I know. Are *you* okay with it?"

There was about a foot between them and Sully stepped forward. "Yeah. You're more than worth it."

"Say it again," Bria sighed inching closer to Sully's body.

"Which part?"

"Any part. I just wanna make sure this is real 'cause I swear I've had a dream like this."

Sully closed the last of the space between them. "So you've been dreaming about me?"

Bria's glossy lips parted on a sigh and she looked up at Sully through her eyelashes. "Every night," she admitted in a heated whisper.

Sully had never felt like this about anyone before. She'd dated women who made her blush and made her stomach flip, women who had her smiling to herself in the middle of a hot, sweaty commute, but she'd never met anyone who made her feel this damn calm. "Can I kiss you?" she breathed.

Bria's excitement was a palpable thing as she stepped forward, pressing her body against Sully's with a giddy insistence. Bria's happiness wound its way through Sully's calm as their lips touched and their tongues slid together.

Sully inhaled Bria's next sigh as she gently held her neck in her hands. Bria's own hands slipped beneath Sully's open shirt and she caressed Sully's torso with shaking fingers. The sun was setting, the air smelled like roasted garlic, and this was the best kiss of Sully's life.

BRIA

Bria had only ever been on a handful of dates and none of them in Sea Port. She'd met a girl from Parkdale at a regional track meet. They ran just okay but consoled one another with milkshakes, fries, and a make out session behind the bleachers right before curfew. They were too young to do anything but email after that, but it signaled to Bria that if she wanted to date, she'd need to leave her hometown. There was no one to be gay with in Sea Port!

Well, no one besides Keith, but besides being queer and single, there wasn't much they could do together. Until now. For the first time in her life, Bria was on a date in Sea Port, but it was off to a questionable start.

Kissing before they even sat down for dinner? Amazing.

Eating at La Bella Rosa? Probably a mistake.

"Welcome," Sal said as soon as Sully pulled the front door open. He was standing behind the hostess stand where Bria normally spent a few evenings a week with a wide grin on his slightly red face and his eyebrows lifted nearly into his hairline.

He knew.

Bria should've expected this. The Sea Port gossip train worked fast, but this blunder was one Bria made all on her own. Even though Sea Port was tiny, she hadn't had time to run home and get changed before her date, so she'd stopped by Sal's apartment above the restaurant. Sal's spare bedroom had been unofficially Bria's for most of her life — a place she could go when her mother worked late or when an event at the restaurant ran too long and she couldn't bear to walk home. Sal was family, and as soon as Sully opened the door for Bria, she could see understanding dawn on his face.

"Please be normal, Sal," she whispered.

"I'm always normal," he said at his regular volume, leaning to the side to smile at Sully.

Bria closed her eyes and took in a deep breath to center herself.

Sully's low chuckle at her back make the hair on her arms stand up. "Hi, Mr. Genova."

"Sully, hello. Hello. How are you?"

"I'm great," she replied. She stopped just behind Bria; her left arm settled against her back. "How are you doing?"

Sal's eyes went immediately to Bria's face and his smile widened. "I'm doing alright."

Bria knew Sal well enough to know what those three words meant. If her mother hadn't heard about her date from Old Ms. Kemp, she'd hear it from Sal, sooner rather than later. Bria would've told her mother about Sully...eventually. She just wanted to enjoy her all to herself for one night, but apparently Sea Port was too small for that kind of privacy.

"Can we get a table, Sal?" she asked politely, biting back a frustrated edge.

"Oh, yes. Yes!" He fumbled grabbing the menus from the stand as if he'd never done it before. "Where do you want to sit?"

Bria took a deep breath before gently taking the menus from Sal's hand. "We'll be at table twelve. Can you bring us some water, please?"

Sal's eyes finally softened and he smiled at her, patting her hand and motioning toward the dining room. "I can do that."

"Follow me," Bria said. Sully nodded gently before stepping behind her with a small smile on her face.

Bria knew this dining room like the back of her hand. She could navigate her way around the tables with her eyes closed. About half the tables were full, which for Sal was a great mid-week turnout, but Bria wanted privacy. She took Sully around the corner to the alcove Sal sometimes called the tunnel of love — an inside joke.

"This okay?" Bria asked as she turned around to find Sully's eyes still on her.

"This is perfect," she breathed, rushing around Bria to pull out her chair. Bria clutched the menus to her chest and sat, shivering when Sully's hands brushed her bare arms.

They sat across from one another, nervously locking eyes and then looking away. Bria felt like a lovesick teenager.

"You gonna read the menu to me?" Sully finally asked.

"Oh shit!" Bria hissed, setting both menus on the table. Sully tried to hand one back.

"I know that thing by heart. Even the typos," she laughed. "You know Sal, right?"

It took Sully a second to answer. "Oh, yeah. We're both in the Sea Port small business work group. He's always been nice to me."

"Sal's nice to everyone," Bria said.

"And you work for him, right?"

Bria nodded. "Sometimes. Now that Mary's giving me more hours, I mostly just help out when he *really* needs me, but I've known Sal all my life. He and my mom have been best friends since they were kids. He's basically family."

"That's sweet," Sully said. Bria nodded as the other woman leaned back in her chair. Their knees bumped under the table and Bria licked her lips while she took a deep breath through her nose.

"So..." Sully smiled. "Since you know the menu so well, what would you recommend?"

Bria let out a loud breath, always happy to share her opinions. "The whole menu's great," she said, because it was, "but I have some suggestions. First and most important is not to order the calamari any way but fried."

A look of horror shifted over Sully's face. "Why?"

"It's better fried," she said quickly. "It arrives frozen and Sal puts it in a few pastas, but fried is best, in my opinion. I didn't mean to scare you. Sorry. I'm just nervous."

Sully's face relaxed again and she shifted in her seat, and this time, more than their knees touched. Bria opened her legs for Sully's knee to move between hers. When their eyes met this time, they didn't look away.

"I'm nervous too," Sully admitted.

"I don't know what you have to be nervous about."

"I want you to like me," she admitted with a nonchalant shrug.

Bria swallowed hard and reached under the table. She moved her hand over Sully's knee. "I already more than like you." She tried to channel Sully's casual tone but her voice shook as she spoke — equal parts nerves and lust.

Sully followed her lead and smoothed her fingers over Bria's bare knee. They both sighed softly while they touched skin to skin.

"Okay! Water for the table," Sal announced before appearing around the small screen separating them from the rest of the dining room.

Bria jumped, pulling her hand away, but Sully's hand remained still, caressing the sensitive skin on the inside of Bria's knee. Sully licked her lips and smirked before lifting her eyes to thank Sal.

It was bad manners for Bria not to acknowledge him but she couldn't bear to take her eyes off Sully. She wasn't even hungry anymore. Not for food, at least.

WELCOME TO SEA PORT

SEVEN

Sully

When Sully moved to Sea Port four years ago, she'd been prepared to have limited dating options, not celibacy. There was a gay bar a few towns over in Juniper Lake. Willie dragged Sully there at least once a quarter, even though they both knew Sully hated the club scene. Sometimes Sully thought they went there so Willie could let her hair down away from the prying eyes of Porties who'd known her all her life, so Sully didn't complain too much. But Juniper Lake trips aside, Sully had been pretty damn lonely for the last few years, and maybe that's why she was just as hungry by the time Sal took their plates away as when they sat down.

"It was good, right?" Bria said excitedly.

Sully nodded, wiping her mouth. "I've been meaning to come here but..."

"But what? There's only so many places to eat in Sea Port."

Sully reached for her water glass and took a deep gulp,

trying to find the right way to say the thing she'd been thinking. But Bria cut her off with another roll of her eyes.

"Let me guess, you were probably thinking an Italian restaurant in this small Southern town in the middle of nowhere would be terrible."

Sully smiled but Bria kept going. "Or maybe you were wondering how Sal even got here."

"Not that last one," Sully laughed. "If I've learned nothing else about Sea Port, it's that this place loves a misfit. It collects the most random people like trading cards."

Bria's face lit up. "That's such a good way of looking at it."

"How did Sal get here?" Sully asked, just wanting to keep Bria talking about anything. About everything.

Bria leaned forward to rest her forearms on the table. Sully clenched her fists under the table and watched Bria speak, trying her hardest not to look at her cleavage. Thankfully, her smile was distracting as hell.

"So, story goes that Sal's grandfather came to the South in the early twentieth century."

"And he moved to Sea Port?"

Bria shook her head quickly. "Nah. He heard about it at some point. Sal doesn't know from who, but when he went back to Italy, he told his family about it."

"Why?" Sully asked.

"No idea!" Bria laughed. "But he did. And when his son and daughter-in-law moved to the States, somehow or other, they ended up here."

"Why?" Sully asked again, laughing this time.

Bria shook her head happily and her twists bounced around her face. "No one knows. Maybe they just wanted to see it so they could tell Sal's granddad. Maybe it was fate. But like you said, Sea Port loves misfits, and two Italian immigrants in the Deep South fit the bill. They came here, decided to stay, opened the restaurant, had Sal, and here we are." She gestured around the restaurant like it was the physical manifestation of Sal's family's dreams, and maybe it was.

Sully could've left Sea Port at any time in the last few years. When she was worried the renovations for her coffee shop would cost more than she could afford, when she was so lonely and horny she couldn't think straight, when it was a hundred degrees before noon, Sully always had the option to pack up her things and go back to Chicago, but she stayed because there was something about Sea Port that just called to her, just like it had called to Sal's grandparents and parents.

Everywhere she looked, there were stories like Sal's of people who came to town looking for something they often couldn't name, but somehow managed to find in Sea Port of all places. In college, Sully had heard stories like Sal's from Willie and she'd been skeptical that a town so small could hold all those dreams, but it did. It still was, including Sully's.

"What about your family?" Sully asked Bria with a nod and a quick glance at her cleavage.

"The Stones are one of the Firsts," she replied with a sheepish grin. "Right there with the Walthams and Freemans and Johnsons and blah-blah, there was a Stone. My granddaddy used to have a farm on the outskirts, but my mom didn't want to run it, so he sold it and bought the house we live in in town. There's even a street named for us, but it doesn't really lead anywhere these days."

Sully sat back in her chair while Bria spoke. She recounted a brief history of her family with a transcendent smile on her face. Sully was listening but she also let herself get lost in Bria's beauty. So lost, the grip she had on her patience slipped away.

As soon as Bria was done speaking, Sully leaned forward and looked her in the eyes. "You can say no," she said in a whisper.

"I'll probably say yes," Bria said quickly.

Lightning moved across Sully's skin. "You want to get out of here?"

"See?" Bria beamed. "Told you so."

Sully immediately pushed up from the table. "Wait," Bria said.

Sully fell back into her seat. "Right, we need the check."

"No, not that. I mean, yes, that, but also, I need to tell you something." Bria's fingers were twisting together on the table.

"What's wrong?" Sully asked.

"Nothing's wrong, technically. I just wanted you to know that I, um... I live with my mom."

"Okay?"

Bria's eyebrows knit together. "That's...it. That's what I wanted to tell you. I live with my mom so, you know, we can't...go...there."

Sully frowned and stared at her for a few more silent seconds before exhaling loudly. "Oh my god, I thought you were going to tell me you have a girlfriend in Juniper Lake or this was some elaborate prank or something."

Bria let out a shocked laugh. "No. I mean, why would I

do that? Also, if it was a prank, wouldn't I have just sat in the main dining room to make it really embarrassing?"

Sully sighed. "*That's* the part your stuck on? Not the girlfriend in Juniper Lake?" She stood from her chair.

Bria tossed her napkin on the table and stood as well. "I haven't been to Juniper Lake in half a decade. The prank was more interesting."

"Is the lesbian community in this county that dead?" Sully laughed.

Bria licked her lips and then stepped close into Sully's side. "Not dead, just hidden in plain sight," she cooed while reaching for Sully's hand and slowly winding their fingers together. Sully's heart was beating so hard and her blood was so loud in her ears that she couldn't think straight for a few seconds.

"We can go to my house," Sully finally said. "I've been dreaming about getting you in my bed for months."

Bria's relieved smile and small nod was all Sully needed to see before she tightened her grip on Bria's hand and pulled her out of their small corner of the restaurant. They needed to pay the bill and get out of here ASAP before they became the next Jonah and Lorraine.

BRIA

B ria loved Sea Port after dark. There wasn't much to do
or see, just empty streets, and on the right night,
nothing but millions of stars in the sky. When they were in
high school, she and Keith used to sneak out of their houses
and meet up in front of the city admin building to just...
wander around town. Small-town things.

But walking these same streets with Sully was different.

The streets were still mostly empty and there were a
couple of streetlamps now thanks to the new Mayor
Waltham, but Sea Port looked about the same as she remembered. Although with Sully by her side, everything looked
better by a mile. Bria opened her mouth to say...something,
but then shut her lips before she could say a word. She
shoved her hand into her bag and pulled out a tin of mints,
immediately popping two into her mouth. She offered the
open package to Sully.

"Garlic is Sal's favorite food group," Bria laughed.

Sully smiled and plucked two mints from the tin just as
they walked under one of the new streetlights. Bria got a
clear image of Sully's tongue as she placed the mints into her
mouth.

The gulp that echoed from Bria's throat sounded loud as
hell to her own ears. "God, you're sexy," she blurted out.

"I was thinking the same thing about you," she replied.

Sully grabbed Bria's hand and pulled her down Main
with an urgency Bria didn't just feel but recognized deep in
her bones. She'd been waiting months for this moment and
the moments that would come next. Happiness didn't feel
like a strong enough emotion to describe how she felt, but it
was the only word that popped into Bria's mind as they

giddily walked to the corner, turned right onto Freedom Way, and sprinted toward Sully's house.

Bria's crush had stopped being something small and incidental — something she forgot when Sully wasn't around — months ago. She didn't know exactly when it happened, but at some point, Bria's crush had become a living thing inside her. She found herself looking for Sully on the street, listening with an intrusive ear for any chatter about her, floating after her Wednesday deliveries. Bria's crush on Sully made her heart beat faster whenever she smelled roasting coffee in the air. Some mornings, she'd crack open her bedroom window to let that scent set the mood as she touched herself.

That didn't feel like just a crush.

Bria nearly tripped over her own feet as Sully led her onto her front porch. The porchlight was dark, but the moon gave Bria more than enough light to see her shadowed profile as she reached into her pocket for her keys. Bria crowded close and lifted onto her toes, letting the tip of her nose graze Sully's jaw, just wanting to smell the bitter scent of coffee on her skin.

Sully squeezed Bria's hand but didn't move otherwise. She didn't unlock her door or push Bria away; she just stood there, waiting for her to make the next move. So, she did.

"Everyone in Sea Port watched me grow up," Bria whispered. Sully's brows dipped in confusion. "I can't walk to work without running into people who remember me when I was in diapers. People treat me like I'm their little sister or niece or daughter, whatever."

"Um...okay?" Sully breathed.

Bria licked her lips and shook her head, trying not to smile just yet. "That's not how I want you to treat me."

It took a second for Sully to catch the softball Bria was lobbing at her. If words hadn't worked, she was prepared to just hike her dress over her hips if need be, but then Sully finally lifted a hand to the side of Bria's face and caressed her hairline with the pad of her thumb.

"How do you want me to treat you, Bria?" Sully's voice was thick with lust.

Bria rubbed her thighs together, squirming with need before leaning forward so she could say these next words directly against Sully's lips.

"I want you to fuck me sweet but a little rough. You don't gotta be too gentle with me," Bria moaned into Sully's mouth.

She'd been waiting months to say those words.

WELCOME TO SEA PORT

EIGHT

Sully

There was only a single lamp at the corner and the warm glow didn't stretch all the way to Sully and Willie's duplex. A comforting darkness swallowed the porch and she happily let the shadows fool her into believing that this little patch of the world was only for her and Bria to share.

Sully left her keys hanging from the lock and wrapped her arms around Bria's waist. She walked her against the railing and leaned down until her fingers brushed her thighs. She let her short nails scrape along Bria's skin, lifting her dress out of the way as she moved.

Sully pressed her mouth against Bria's lips as she gasped. She wanted to taste surprise on her tongue.

"Like that?" she whispered into Bria's mouth.

"Yeah," Bria moaned.

Sully teased her for a little bit longer, mixing her rough grip with gentle circles while she kissed and licked Bria from her mouth to the base of her neck. She could've stayed there all night, just touching and kissing her until the sun came up, but Bria had other plans.

"Unless you're tryna eat me out on your welcome mat, maybe we should go inside," she whimpered.

She smiled against Bria's pulse. "Is that an option?"

Sully thought Bria's laughter sounded better when she could feel it against her chest.

She loosened her grip on Bria by degrees but grabbed her hand as she turned back to her front door.

"After you," Sully breathed, reaching inside to flip the light switch just inside her entryway.

Bria bit her bottom lip and led Sully inside, hopefully not for the last time.

Sully closed the door behind them, then wrapped her arm around Bria's waist and pulled her back. She pressed her face into Bria's neck and smelled her skin — brown sugar and citrus.

"Is Mary bringing the chocolate orange donut holes back?" Sully whispered into the crevice of Bria's neck.

"Yeah, how did you know?"

"You smell like the bakery," Sully laughed.

"No, I don't. I showered."

Sully smoothed her hand over Bria's stomach. "Don't matter," she said, kissing the words up Bria's neck. "At this point, you got sugar in your DNA. You can't scrub that off. Thank god." Sully moaned those last two words into Bria's ear while her hand moved between her legs.

"Does that mean you like it?" Bria moaned in soft panting breaths.

"Yeah."

"Good, 'cause I love the way you smell. I never thought the scent of roasted coffee could make me wet."

Now normally, that kinda hyperbole would've been cute, an innocent little white lie a woman tells in the heat of the moment. Except Sully's fingers were between Bria's legs and she could feel the heat radiating through the damp cotton covering her pussy, so Sully knew she wasn't lying.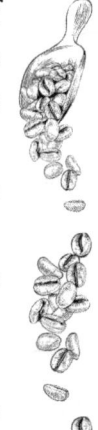

"Goddamn," she moaned just before Bria's mouth covered her lips.

Bria turned in Sully's hold and pressed her against the door. "Bedroom?"

"Upstairs."

They tasted one another for a moment longer, hands roaming and bodies pressed together. Sully turned Bria toward the stairs and wrapped herself possessively around her back. They walked together, moving in slow, measured steps up the stairs and down the hall to Sully's bedroom, their breaths, hearts, and steps in sync.

As soon as they walked into the bedroom, Bria turned in Sully's arms again, her mouth searching as if those few seconds apart had been too long. Because it had been.

Sully couldn't keep her hands still, wanting, needing to feel every part of Bria. Her firm butt, the slope of her back, a soft roll just above her underwear, the curve of her breasts and the lace pattern over her bra cups, all through her thin dress until finally,  she bunched the hem of Bria's dress in her fists and pulled it up her body. They only broke their kiss to get naked. Nothing else could have stopped them from devouring one another whole.

Sully was still holding Bria's dress over their heads when she felt Bria's hands pushing her shirt off her shoulders.

They laughed and kissed as they shed one piece of clothing after another until there was nothing left between them.

And everything left to explore.

They crawled into bed together, meeting in the middle on their knees.

"Can I?" Sully asked, reaching for Bria's chest. Bria pulled Sully's hand to her breasts, sighing happily into her touch.

Her skin was soft and warm under Sully's fingers as she explored the weight, her hard nipples, the soft flesh over her ribs.

Sully circled Bria's areola, fingers closing around her nipple until a shiver ran through her body. Bria grasped her own breasts and squeezed as Sully's hands moved down her stomach. They locked eyes as Sully's fingers slipped into the soft curls over her mound. She inched her knees apart and held her breath while Sully tried to memorize every inch of Bria's face the first time she touched her pussy.

"I can't believe you're this wet," Sully whispered.

"I've been waiting for this," Bria moaned.

Sully pulled her close. "I know the feeling." Her fingers dipped into Bria's wetness, just enough to whet their appetite. Sully sat back on her heels and guided Bria's legs around her thigh until she could set her wet cleft right onto her bare leg. Their relieved groans came out in one gentle breath.

Bria's hands caressed the sides of her face while Sully gripped her waist and started moving her in slow circles up and down. Their heated moans ate up the silence in the empty room. Bria kissed Sully like she wanted to inhale her, devour her entirely. And for the record, Sully wanted that more than anything.

They fell onto the bed, legs still twisted together, Sully's thigh wet from her release. Bria wrapped her arms around her shoulders as they ground against one another and drank their shared moans. Sully sucked Bria's bottom lip into her mouth. Eventually, her lips traveled from Bria's mouth to her jaw, down her neck, soft kisses across her chest and more insistent tastes around her breasts until she finally, *finally* took one of Bria's nipples into her mouth.

"Wait," Bria cried out, shivering from head to toe.

Sully pulled back. "What's wrong?"

Bria laughed and touched the bun at the back of Sully's head. "I love your hair when it's down," she whispered.

Sully wasn't precious about her long, curly hair, but other people were, and it had always made her uncomfortable. It had taken years of therapy to undo an entire childhood of people fawning over her loose wavy strands, light brown skin, and small nose, learning to separate other people's expectations of her from her own. She'd spent thousands of dollars just to be able to look in a mirror and see herself, not who other people thought she was. Most days she didn't have the time or energy to think too much about her hair, let alone what she wore to work. She put her curls in a neat bun every morning so it was out of the way and went on about her life. Letting go of that preoccupation was freeing, but every now and then, when the café crowd was thin, she pulled her hair from the bun and let the air touch her scalp.

But if she'd known Bria liked it, she would've worn it down on Wednesdays, at least.

She turned Bria onto her back and shifted to her knees. She waited while Bria rearranged her head on the pillows, until she had all her attention, before she moved her hands to the back of her head and unwound her bun in careful movements.

She tossed her ponytail holder on the bedside table and then bent over Bria's body.

Bria touched the ends of Sully's hair carefully.

"Better?" Sully asked.

Bria's brow furrowed and she tipped her chin in Sully's direction. "You're perfect no matter how you wear your hair," she said. "I just want to scratch at your scalp while you eat me out."

A reasonable request if there ever was one.

Sully kissed her way down her body, over her shoulders, down her arms, across her hips. Bria gently massaged Sully's scalp, gasping and moaning as she tasted her skin.

She smoothed her hands up Bria's inner thighs as she settled between her legs. Her fingers explored Bria's lips, teasing them apart, circling her clit before moving toward her opening.

Bria's fingers flexed in Sully's hair, dug gently into her scalp, and then she tugged as Sully's fingers slipped deep inside her pussy.

BRIA

S ully had become Bria's private obsession. Every night after work, she'd rush home just to get into bed and giddily return to an imaginary world where she could be with the version of Sully she'd created in her mind. The real thing was so much better.

Sully was watching her as she slipped a third finger inside her. It wasn't just her touch; it was the intensity of her gaze, the way Sully's other hand caressed her hips while she moved her fingers in and out of her sex.

Bria's back arched from the bed and Sully's fingers stilled. Bria didn't want to close her eyes but the tremor was too strong, so she dug her fingers into Sully's hair and let it move through her while Sully's hold on her hips anchored her to the bed. Meanwhile her entire soul drifted away in ecstasy.

By the time Bria's body relaxed, Sully started moving again, although this time her mouth joined her fingers and Bria's back rounded. She managed to open her eyes in just enough time to see Sully's tongue move through her folds and up to her clit. She just barely bit back a moan that might've woken half the neighborhood.

"You don't need to be quiet," Sully whispered against Bria's wet lips.

"Fuck, you're sexy," Bria gasped, spreading her thighs wider.

"There aren't even words for how sexy you are," Sully sighed before lowering her mouth to Bria's sex again.

She couldn't have stifled the next moan if she tried.

Sully tasted every inch of Bria until she had to hold her hips to the mattress, she was shaking so hard. Bria was close to coming again, but then Sully pulled back abruptly.

"Wait," Bria whined.

"What's wrong?"

Bria dug her hands deeper into Sully's strands and pulled her up her body. Their mouths crashed together on twin soft moans while Sully's fingers started moving again. She fucked her in slow, firm thrusts of her hand while they poured all these months of longing into this kiss. Bria carefully extracted her fingers from Sully's hair and the soft cloud fell over them. A light floral smell clung to the edges of that same bitter coffee scent Bria had come to love.

She wrapped her right leg around Sully's waist, pulling her down as she rode her hand in frantic thrusts.

"There you go," Sully whispered. "Your pussy is so fucking soft."

Bria's legs started shaking first, but by the time that next orgasm ripped through her, she was holding onto Sully for dear life and cursing into her hair.

Bria shook in her arms as Sully kissed a path over her chin, down her neck, and across the full length of her collarbone. Her kisses were chaste until her mouth brushed Bria's breasts. Another spasm tickled Bria's spine as Sully's lips, tongue, and teeth grazed her nipples. She lingered just long enough on each nipple, the curve of each breast, and even the sensitive patch of skin underneath that Bria was nearing another orgasm by the time Sully finally pulled her fingers from her pussy.

She felt like her body was falling apart at a cellular level, but all she could do was moan weakly. She eventually managed to pull herself onto her elbows, all so she could watch through hooded eyes as Sully kissed her way back down her body.

"Fuck," she whispered and felt Sully's smile against her rib cage.

Sully left a few pecks around her belly button and then she rubbed her nose along the soft, curly hair above Bria's mound. Bria spread her legs as Sully planted gentle kisses across her inner thighs, the crease of her legs, and the bottom curve of her stomach. Everywhere but where Bria needed her mouth most.

"Please," she whispered when she was finally at the end of her rope.

Sully ran both hands down her inner thighs and smoothed her thumbs along her wet cleft. "Ask me again. Just like that."

Bria tried to squeeze her legs together but Sully was in the way, staring at her hungrily, licking the taste of Bria's skin off her lips, waiting.

"Please," Bria whispered, sounding even more desperate than before.

Sully didn't respond with words, but she did lower herself over Bria's pussy, breathing her in for a few seconds before covering her hooded clit with her mouth. Bria's body bucked sharply at the touch, her legs shaking in Sully's hands. And when she flattened her tongue along the length of her slit, Bria fell back onto the bed thankful that the night was still very young.

She'd dreamed about being naked in Sully's bed. She'd touched herself dozens of times fantasizing about letting Sully do whatever she wanted to her. Hell, she'd once had to catch herself at church when she was just about to pray for a moment like this. Apparently, God sometimes answered prayers she was too blasphemous to speak aloud.

They lost track of time.

All Bria could do was pant and moan and shiver as one orgasm split her open at the center of her core, followed by another. And another. She tried to ground herself in the moment with a firm grip on her own breasts, roughly pinching her nipples, only to fly apart again. Her own touch didn't do much besides make her come harder, which pleased them both.

When Sully finally released her iron grip on Bria's thighs, it was only to work her hands between the bed and Bria's ass and lift her pussy to her mouth so she could eat her like a woman starved.

Bria felt open and exposed and sexier than she'd ever felt in her life, but her throat was too hoarse to say any of that. Besides, she was too busy coming all over Sully's mouth again.

This was hands down the best date of her life.

When Sully finally crawled back up the bed to lie beside her, Bria felt like a rag doll — boneless and entirely Sully's to play with.

"Hey," Sully whispered, her wet fingers tracing circles around Bria's left nipple.

She opened her eyes and Sully smiled shyly with her chin still wet from Bria's release. The absurdity of the moment knocked something loose inside Bria's chest; she started giggling and couldn't stop.

She reached for Sully with shaking hands and pulled her on top of her body. Their tongues tangled together in a deep kiss while their hands explored one another again. They stayed in that kiss for long, quiet moments, tasting one another until Bria's body was back under her own control.

Bria's fingers ghosted under Sully's breasts and down her sides before her arm snaked between Sully's legs. They had all night, so she touched Sully as lazily as she had touched her. She ran her fingers through the soft downy hair there, circled her clit until Sully moaned into her mouth, and then pulled back. Sully watched with hooded eyes as Bria slipped her middle and ring fingers along her tongue before her hand was between their bodies again. Her wet digits brushed Sully's strong thighs briefly before tracing more slow circles over her clit.

"Now it's your turn to beg," Bria whispered, pecking the corner of Sully's mouth while her fingers slid between her soft folds.

Sully's laughter tasted like pure joy on Bria's tongue. "Please," she whispered, rocking her hips into Bria's slow, invading fingers.

Bria gave Sully everything she had given her and more; all the things she'd been dreaming about. She fucked her fingers deep inside while her thumb circled her clit. She kissed Sully until the other woman was a shivering mess on top of her, too busy moaning to kiss her back. Undeterred, Bria tasted Sully's chin, her cheek, her chest, literally anywhere her mouth could touch, wanting to memorize every inch of her skin.

She inserted another finger. "Another," Sully cried out, and Bria happily obliged.

Their limbs were a tangled mess as they humped into one another until Sully lifted onto her knees and Bria slithered under her body, sucking at one breast and then the other while Sully ground onto her fingers. She shut her eyes tight as hot tears slipped from the corners.

The sound of Sully's wet sex filled the room; a sound Bria would never let herself forget.

Bria wiped away those tears with one hand while circling Sully's clit with the other, hoping with all her heart that Sully could see how much she wanted to care for her in this touch.

Eventually Sully fell onto the bed at her side, out of breath but still laughing happily. Bria moved over her, equally elated, kissing at her warm face.

"Is it too late to ask you for another date?" Sully laughed.

"About fucking time," Bria whispered, slipping her tongue into Sully's mouth.

Question asked and answered.

WELCOME TO SEA PORT

Willie never wanted to be Mayor of Sea Port, but public service was in her blood.

She left home for college but also feeling deeply conflicted about her family's expectations, especially her father's. It made sense, then, that her father was the reason she came back. Willie wanted to make sure there was another Mayor Waltham in Sea Port, not because she wanted the job so much as she wanted to make sure there would be a Sea Port for future generations to inherit.

No one had been happier that Willie decided to run for office than her mother. She'd been preparing for this probably since Willie was in the womb, so she'd been ready to extract a few promises before the campaign began.

First, and most confusingly, she'd had to reassure the entire Waltham family that she wasn't doing this because of her father. Maybe if she'd moved back before he died, she might've had an easier time on this front, but the thing about rushing home to say goodbye was that everything after that was colored by her grief. They'd all expected her to take up the mayoral office because she was her daddy's daughter, but somehow, when faced with the natural conclusion of her father's influence on her young life, they were worried about her living for his memory rather than herself. Contradictory messaging be damned, apparently.

As Skip Waltham's only child and the future of two old Portie families, continuing the family's legacy was an expectation, but no Waltham wanted Willie to do it out of obligation alone — that was why leaving for college had always been part of the plan. Her parents wanted her to leave the South to acquire the skills and connections she needed to lead their small town into the future. Willie just wanted the opportunity to become her own woman. They all got what they wanted in the end. By the time grief pulled Willie back to Sea Port, she'd lived the life she wanted and was ready to live the life her family and the town expected.

The second promise her mother had extracted was that Willie could only run for mayor if she refused to let the town elders bully her. Easier said than done, but Willie made the promise anyway. The last four years as Sea Port's Mayor were tricky, but she was coming into her own. Sure, she still had to take deep breaths to settle her nerves before every City Council meeting, and sometimes she was tempted by the offer to sit on someone's porch with a cool glass of lemonade and a slice of crumb cake like she used to, but she was surviving.

She was a Waltham after all.

The third promise Willie's mother extracted was to make

the mayor's office her own...if she was elected. They'd both laughed softly at that last-minute addition before Willie had agreed, thinking it would be easy. She'd always been head-strong and opinionated; qualities her parents had taught her, even if it made raising her harder for them. But the first time she stepped into the mayor's office after her election, she understood what her mother had been trying to communi-cate. Willie had spent her entire life in that office — coloring at a small desk her father set up in the corner just for her, dropping by after school just to say hey; thousands of tiny daily interactions, most of which she couldn't even remem-ber. Her father's office — the mayor's office — was like an extension of her home, and when she stepped into it as an adult, just months after his death, she still thought of it that way — *his* office. Not hers.

Those first few weeks had been a mindfuck. Whenever a new problem landed on her desk, her first instinct was to ask herself what her father would do. How could she not? She was headstrong, opinionated, a daddy's girl, and grieving the second greatest loss of her life.

Thankfully, Sea Port's dire straits had kept Willie on track. Sea Port couldn't afford for her to flounder. If she believed her own family lore, Sea Port needed a Mayor Waltham to get them through this hurdle. The problem for Willie was the fear that she was the wrong Waltham for the job.

"Your father was a good mayor," her mother said. "Old. Fair. And male. Be better than him." That advice had made Willie nearly fall apart in laughter with tears streaming down her face, glee and despair warring in her chest.

And lastly, but most relevant to this morning, Willie had

promised her mother not to let the job become her whole life. Her father had done that and it had taken a toll on their marriage, no matter how hard they'd tried to hide it.

Of all the people who would be disappointed that the sun was peeking over the horizon as Willie walked home from her office in yesterday's pantsuit with a crick in her neck, her mother would've been top of the list. Willie was second. Maybe third, actually, because Sully wouldn't be too happy about this either.

She hadn't meant to fall asleep at her desk. She'd been going over the city's budget and working through applications for new Transplant house requests and relocation assistance when suddenly, it was morning and there was a piece of paper stuck to her face.

She scurried home with her mother's voice in her head telling her that this was how it started. If she didn't check herself, she'd be keeping a spare suit in the closet behind her desk — like her dad did — and a full set of her toiletries in the bottom drawer of her desk — just like him — and then next thing she knew, she'd be waving off signs of a heart attack at her own peril. Just like her father.

A warning Willie knew she should heed, but couldn't.

All she wanted was a quick nap in her own bed and a scalding hot shower. She rushed home, praying no one from WAKC would see her and rat her out to her mother.

Sometimes, Willie couldn't believe she was back in her hometown. She'd spent practically her entire childhood champing at the bit to be anywhere else — New York, London, Tokyo, cities so big most people didn't know all their neighbors' names, let alone the names of their entire families going back two generations, at least. But then sometimes, she found herself power walking along Sea Port's quaint, deserted streets just before dawn, shocked she'd ever left because this was where she belonged.

Willie reached over the gap and flipped the latch on the low picket fence at the duplex she shared with Sully. She stepped onto the paved pathway and started rummaging around in her purse for her keys. She'd just set her foot onto the bottom step when the sound of a door opening pulled her attention up the porch.

Instead of her best friend glaring at her from a cracked door, Willie saw Bria stepping onto the porch, pulling Sully's front door closed slowly, teeth gritted as she tried not to make too much noise. Willie took a step back, her mouth fell open, and then she froze, one hand still shoved deep inside her bag.

She would know those short, neat twists anywhere; they'd become her particular obsession over the past few months. She was too tired to pull on the Waltham mask, so she watched Bria in shocked confusion.

Bria closed the door and let out a triumphant sigh. When she turned around and saw Willie standing at the bottom of the stairs, she yelped and jumped back into Sully's door. "Shit," she whispered, stepping quickly away.

Her small cry kick-started Willie's brain and she put on a weak version of her mayoral smile; a smile hardwired into her brain since childhood. "Sorry," she whispered.

Bria shook her head and laughed softly. "No, I'm sorry. I just didn't expect anyone to be out here this early."

"Neither did I," Willie admitted. There were *so many* things she wanted to say — things she'd been thinking of saying for months — but they all flew out of her head.

"Leaving so soon?" she asked, nodding toward Sully's door.

Bria ducked her head, smiling wider. "I gotta get changed for work." She looked at her watch and grimaced, finally moving forward, bouncing down the steps.

Willie wasn't often rendered speechless, but she watched Bria with a lump in her throat — a lump that refused to shift enough for her to speak.

"See ya, Mayor Waltham," Bria called as she passed by with a quick wave.

Willie managed to wave back as Bria opened and closed her gate. And then she retraced her steps toward the sidewalk, but only so she could watch Bria walk down Freedom toward Main. If Bria turned right at the corner, she could walk two more blocks and arrive at the house where Willie's mother and father, the late Mayor Skip Waltham, had lived. But Willie knew Bria's path would take her left at the corner. She'd walk a few more blocks until she got to Main and Opal Avenue. There, she'd cross the street and walk one more block to arrive at her own house, where she still lived with her mother. Willie had mapped the route herself. As Bria bounced away, Willie stared at the empty streets feeling wearier than ever. Rather than deserted and quaint, the streets she loved felt haunted by ghosts.

When Bria was out of sight, Willie turned back to the condo with a heavy heart and heavier steps. She hesitated on the porch, her gaze shifting toward Sully's door. She considered letting herself inside her best friend's home and finally having a conversation she should've had weeks ago, but it was too early and she was too tired.

She let herself into her condo with a sigh, kicked her

shoes off at the door, and walked up to her bedroom like a zombie. She stripped down to her underwear and crawled under her covers.

Her alarm would go off in a couple of hours, but that was a problem for later.

And so was Bria.

WELCOME TO SEA PORT

TEN

Bria

By all rights, Bria should've been exhausted. She'd spent the entire night talking and laughing and touching Sully. One night couldn't make up for over a year of yearning, but they tried their hardest. She managed a couple hours of sleep before the internal alarm clock she'd developed while working at Confections yanked her into consciousness. She rushed home to get ready for another busy morning at the bakery feeling exhilarated. Like she could do damn near anything.

Even though Bria had a bit of a reputation around town, she'd never once had to rush home just before dawn in last night's clothes. She wished she'd had the opportunity for those kinds of youthful scandals, but small-town living and all that. Although, Bria's walk of shame had her thinking that maybe small-town Sea Port was changing for real.

No coffee or sugar rush had ever felt this good.

She did have to jog the last couple of blocks to get into

Confections on time...ish. Mary could be a bit of a taskmaster, but the only part of her job she was completely lax about was on what time they started in the morning. As long as there was at least one batch of donuts in the display case by five-thirty, they'd at least survive the morning rush.

Some days, Bria unlocked the back door and the sound of Mary's Sugar Rush '90s pop playlist slapped her in the face. She'd find Mary doing a little two-step over blueberry muffin batter, drop her bag in the office, wash her hands, and jump in. And some mornings, she'd step into a dark, cold kitchen and work in complete silence until the coffee kicked in. It worked for them, but this morning, Bria was definitely cutting it close.

She started apologizing as soon as she unlocked the back door but found the kitchen empty. Bria let out a relieved sigh and then got to work. She was just tying her apron strings behind her back when Mary stepped through the back door, already singing. In no time, they fell into their regular morning routine with Bria trying not to randomly blurt out the details of her night to Mary or the cinnamon roll dough, whoever was willing to listen.

Bria slid the last tray of donuts into the display case right on time to open. She jogged around the counter to unlock the front door only to come face-to-face with her mother.

She took a few steps back into the storefront as Evelyn stepped inside with her right eyebrow arched into her hairline.

Bria had become *very* acquainted with this particular look in middle school. It didn't have a fixed translation. Depending on the time of day, her mother's mood, and the severity of Bria's transgression, that look could mean anything from "Excuse me...?" to "Little girl, don't make me..." It was surprisingly flexible, but it only really had one goal: scare the living shit out of Bria. And it worked. Still.

"Mornin', mama. What're you doing here?"

"Good morning. I'm here to make sure my only child is alive." There wasn't anyone in the world Bria feared more than her mother, but she was also her mom's biggest fan, even when she was doing the most.

"Mama, stop being dramatic," Bria said, rolling her eyes. "Nothing happens in Sea Port."

"Exactly," Evelyn replied, hands on hips. "Which is why I was shocked you didn't come home last night."

Bria pressed her mouth shut, but her mind went immediately to a shadowy image of Sully's head between her legs. Her skin was hot from embarrassment even thinking about last night in this moment, and she started squirming under her mother's critical but loving eye.

"Well? I'm waiting."

"I'm an adult, mama."

"An adult who still lives under my roof."

Bria was operating off a few hours' sleep and three donut holes, not nearly enough fuel to deal with her mother, so she gave in, turning on her heels. "I was out with a friend," she said, hoping against all hope her mother would take the hint and end this conversation right there.

She didn't.

Evelyn walked up to the cash register with pursed lips. "Yes, I heard."

"You talked to Sal?" Bria gasped.

Her mother had both eyebrows raised now in a silent

challenge. This look only had one real translation. *Come on. I dare you to lie to me.* Younger Bria had liked the gamble of the double eyebrow extension, but she was grown now and wasn't interested in getting grounded at work.

"Fine," she said, rolling her eyes. "I was on a date."

Her mother's grimace flattened into a smile that pushed her plump cheeks high. "Is it that woman from the coffee shop you've been after for all these months?" She was so excited her words were practically tripping over one another.

"I wasn't *after* her," Bria hissed.

"Sure, baby. Whatever you say." She was practically glowing. "I'm assuming it went very well?"

"Not gonna answer that," Bria said, fighting to keep last night far from her thoughts.

"You not coming home last night already did." Evelyn smirked.

The bell over the shop door jingled as Mrs. Petersen pushed inside.

"Can we talk about this tonight?" Bria whispered to her mother.

"Oh? Will you be home tonight?" Her face was soft with glee.

Bria couldn't roll her eyes hard enough. "You're terrible, you know that?"

"Where do you think you got it from? Now give me an assorted dozen, I'm gonna be late for work."

Bria pulled an empty box from the shelf under the register and started working on her mother's order.

"Make sure you give your mama the best," Evelyn chided softly.

Bria sighed. "Mama, they're all good. I made them."

"Yes, you did," Evelyn whispered proudly. "My baby made these," she said in a voice loud enough for Mrs. Petersen to hear.

SULLY

Sully was supposed to be working on the coffee shop's quarterly budget. She had a flat white to her left, the last two quarters of ledgers open on her computer, and her entire day cleared to get it all done.

Willie forced her to take some small-business seminars before she'd opened her coffee shop. Technically, the classes were part of the Sea Port Relocation Initiative's support for new businesses, but really, Willie had used her for market research to choose the best program for new business owners who had a great idea but were totally out of their depth like Sully had been. She'd learned some good habits and she was trying hard to stick to them, but her budgeting dates were the worst, especially this one, because she couldn't concentrate to save her life this morning.

She'd been sitting in the small, disorganized closet next to the storeroom that she used for her office, staring at the same page of her expense sheet for at least the last twenty minutes. She could see the numbers; she just couldn't process any of the information because all she could think about was last night. *Bria.*

A small part of Sully had hoped that finally getting a literal taste of Bria might ease the intensity of her feelings, but it hadn't. Not one bit. Sully couldn't think about her budget when Bria was just a few blocks away.

This was going to be a long day.

"Girl, get it the fuck together," she muttered to herself and sat up straight in her chair, reaching for her coffee cup. She took a sip of lukewarm coffee and frowned. She seriously considered going out front to get a fresh cup, but it would be a slippery slope. One second, she'd be just popping behind the counter to make her drink, the next she'd get to talking with someone in line or start cleaning the workstation and next thing she knew, it would be the end of the day and her budget would still be unfinished. So, she choked down another sad sip of room temperature coffee and scrolled to the top of her expenditures sheet.

As soon as she started scanning the figures, someone knocked on the door.

"I'm busy," she called. The doorknob turned and Sully knew exactly who was on the other side as she rolled her eyes.

Willie pushed the door open and stood in the doorway.

"I said I'm busy," Sully sighed, leaning back in her chair.

"I heard you," Willie replied. She was wearing a classy pair of black wide-leg slacks and a cream cashmere sweater, a far cry from the girl with long black and purple braids the day they met. They stared at one another while Sully waited for Willie to move. It didn't happen.

"What are you doing here?" Sully asked.

Instead of responding, Willie sucked her bottom lip into her mouth and started chewing, piquing Sully's interest. She squinted up at her best friend and noticed details she hadn't at first glance, like the dark circles under Willie's eyes and the small smudge of lipstick on her chin. But mostly it was the fact that Willie seemed to be at a loss for words. Sully had never seen that before.

She stood from her desk and looked down at her own outfit — baggy jeans and an old band t-shirt, the difference in clothing perfectly encapsulating their personalities. "What's up?"

Willie chewed on her lip for another few seconds before releasing it with a small sigh. "You got a second?"

"Of course." It was so unlike Willie to even ask the question. "What's wrong?"

She would've offered Willie a seat if there was one, but this office was only big enough for her, a small desk, a skinny file cabinet, and overflow boxes of recycled paper cups. She was just about to suggest they go out to the café when Willie stepped into her cloffice and closed the door behind her before she could even speak. The room was cramped already and with Willie squeezing in, it was nearly claustrophobic.

"I need to talk to you about something," Willie said, twisting her fingers together.

"We're talking."

"I don't know where to start," Willie whispered, almost to herself.

"How about the beginning?"

Willie looked all over the room for a second before making eye contact again. "I accidentally fell asleep in my office last night."

Sully rolled her eyes. "How many times do I have to tell you to stop doing that?"

"I said it was an accident."

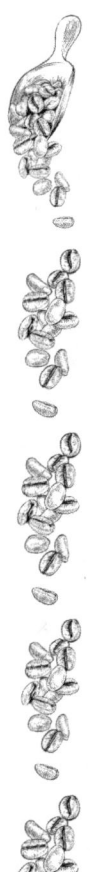

"There are accidents and then there are expected consequences of your actions and choices."

"You sound like my mother," Willie said, frowning deeply.

"Well, she's smart, so..." Sully fired back, letting the implication hang in the air. "Also, she makes the best apple pie I've ever had in my life. Actually—"

Willie shook her head and held up a hand. "Let's stay on track." Sully pressed her lips shut and nodded once. "So anyway, I woke up this morning and walked home and I... I, um, ran into Bria Stone coming out of your place."

"Okay?" Sully's voice sounded bored, but inside she was soft and gooey at just hearing Bria's name. Heat spread across her cheeks like wildfire. She was down bad.

Willie's serious tone yanked her from her memories. "Lisa, I need you to do me a favor," she said.

Sully hated her first name, Willie knew that. "You're not framing this request well, but I'm listening." Sully's voice was hard and frustrated.

Willie's mouth flattened into a hard line and she nodded slowly. "I hate to do this," she whispered, "but I need you to nip whatever is going on between you two in the bud."

"No," Sully spat out.

Willie's face was stricken. Sully never told Willie no. "Hear me out."

Sully shrugged but didn't give her an inch. "I'm listening."

Sully didn't think there was anything Willie could say to change her mind, but for her, she'd listen at the very least. But Willie didn't explain herself. Instead, she shook her head and clenched and released her fists before crossing her arms across her chest, mirroring Sully's stance.

"Actually, no, can you just do this for me? Please?"

"Why?" Sully bit out. She could feel herself about to get angry, so she took a deep breath to regulate her breathing.

"I can't explain it to you. Not right now," Willie said, a slight pleading tone in her voice. Willie didn't plead, beg, or whine. Ever. She was a Waltham.

Sully took another breath and closed her eyes. She could feel beads of angry sweat on her upper lip and at the small of her back. She opened her eyes and glared at her best friend. "Explain yourself."

Willie shook her head on impulse.

As a life rule, Sully didn't believe in ultimatums. She believed in healthy communication and compromise. Willie was different. Maybe it was the consequence of being raised by a politician or maybe it was just because she was stubborn as an ox, but over the years, Sully had learned that sometimes she needed to shake her — metaphorically — to get at the truth.

"I love you," Sully started. "Which is why I'm giving you two minutes to tell me what the fuck this is all about."

"Sully..." Willie started, but Sully held up a hand, cutting her off.

"I'm not one of your constituents—" Sully started.

"Technically..." Willie tried to interject.

"*Technically,* I'm the girl who taught you how to use a tampon. I'm the one who held your hair back when you threw up after the club. The one who held you while you cried all night after your father died. I'm your family."

"You are," Willie said. "That's why I'm coming to you."

"With nothing," Sully shot back. "Just a request for me to break it off with the first person I've liked in years. The girl I've been crushing on for nearly two years? If you even want me to consider that, I'm gonna need more than sad eyes."

She was a little out of breath by the time she finished and at some point while she was speaking — ranting? — Sully started shouting. Not like full-on yelling, but definitely louder than her tiny little office could reasonably accommodate.

"Two years?" Willie asked in a small voice. "You've had a crush on her for that long?"

"Yes," Sully ground out. "And if you were a better friend, you'd have known that."

Willie sucked in a sharp breath, pain etched on her face. Sully hadn't meant to make her cry, but she realized as soon as she said those words that they were her true feelings even if they were unfair. She'd moved to Sea Port knowing that Willie would be busy and their relationship would change, but not this much. She hadn't known the loneliness of living in such a small town even when her best friend lived right next door. When she wasn't busy, Willie was, and vice versa. Their time together was short, and it hurt Sully more than she'd ever said. Seeing that it also hurt Willie was a small comfort, but that tiny consolation all but disappeared as tears spilled down Willie's cheeks.

Sully sighed and walked toward Willie, pulling her into a hug. She was pissed, not heartless. Willie wrapped her arms around Sully's waist and they held onto one another until Willie's soft sniffles were the only sound in the room.

"She's my sister," Willie whispered in a voice barely audible even as they embraced one another.

Sully froze and leaned back from their embrace. "Say what?"

"My father had an affair with her mother. Bria's my sister."

Sully's mouth fell open. "Holy shit!"

WELCOME TO SEA PORT

ELEVEN

Bria

It was a slow afternoon in the bakery. Once the morning rush passed and the shelves were refilled, Bria and Charlie had spent their downtime watching the goings-on in their little slice of downtown through the big picture windows. It was boring, but they were both used to it. And considering how little sleep she'd gotten last night, Bria didn't complain.

A year ago, Bria would've freaked out at every dip in the flow of customers, worried she was watching her job disappear right in front of her eyes. But after a few years and many teacakes sold, she at least knew that Mary would fire Charlie before her any day.

"Stop thinking about getting me fired," Charlie sighed, leaning against the back of the display case, her chin resting on her folded forearms.

"I wasn't plotting on you," Bria said. "Just thinking."
"About?"
Bria smiled. "Last hired, first fired."

Charlie whirled on her and, in one smooth motion, snatched the towel they all kept in the strings of their aprons and flung it at Bria.

"Bitch," Charlie hissed.

"I'll write you a good recommendation," Bria laughed, tossing the towel back.

Charlie looked like she was about to unleash every curse word she knew, but the front door opened and the bell chimed, cutting her off.

"Welcome to—" they both started to say, stopping when they saw Santos stepping into the shop.

"Oh, you," Charlie said.

"Charlie!" Bria hissed.

Santos lifted an eyebrow but didn't otherwise respond. He nodded in Bria's direction as he stepped into the service area and into the kitchen. Once he was out of sight, they turned back to the window just in time to see Mr. Lee's old tan Ford truck cross their view.

"Think he's coming here or the Sunnyside?" Charlie asked.

"Both," Bria said, stifling a yawn. "We don't replenish the pie at the diner until tomorrow."

"Nice," Charlie said, covering her mouth to hide her own yawn.

They stared through the window for a few more silent moments and then jumped at the sound of Mary's barely contained shout. Bria and Charlie turned to one another with raised eyebrows.

"I said no. Drop it!" Mary yelled. At Santos.

Bria's mouth fell open. Mary could be loud — very loud, actually — but she never yelled. And she certainly never yelled at Knox or Santos. Well, not yelling in a bad way. Bria and Charlie stared at one another in shock. Well, Bria was shocked; Charlie looked like she was ready to belly crawl across the bakery to the kitchen door to hear them clearly.

"Don't," Bria warned to the only person under forty-three ready, willing, and able to join WAKC. Her invitation had to be in the mail.

When they hadn't been staring into small-town oblivion, Charlie had been trying to pump Bria for details on her date with Sully while Bria had been trying to figure out how the hell she even knew about that. Charlie forgot Bria entirely at the sound of Mary's voice and started tiptoeing toward the kitchen.

"Charlie, stop," Bria hissed, grabbing at her arm, but the other woman shrugged her off and shushed her at the same time.

She shook her head. "I've been waiting for this to come to a head."

"Waiting for what? No," Bria said, shaking her head. "Don't answer that. Whatever's going on with them is none of our business."

Charlie reared back as if Bria's words had actually hurt her. "None of our...business?" Her voice was a pained whisper. Bria rolled her eyes and then stared at Charlie, who stared right back while the muffled timbre of Santos's deep voice filtered into the quiet storefront.

Bria sighed. "Fine, what's going on?"

Charlie's face lit up and she rushed back to Bria's side, speaking in excited whispers. "Okay, so here's what I've picked up so far. Santos and Knox want Mary to go to Denver to meet Santos's family."

"Aww," Bria sighed.

"I know!" Charlie beamed. "And then after Denver, they were thinking of going to meet Mary's people."

"What about Knox?"

Charlie shrugged. "It hasn't come up yet."

"So Mary doesn't want to meet Santos's family?"

"No, I think she was down for that, but she doesn't want to take them to meet hers."

"Why not?"

Charlie rolled her eyes. "If you'd shut up, I might be able to find out."

Bria pursed her lips, ready to tell her off, but then Santos pushed the swinging door open so hard it slammed into the rack they kept for cooled and packed phone orders. They jumped at the loud racket of thankfully empty trays clattering to the floor. Both women turned back to the front window with wide eyes, watching Santos in their peripheral vision. He stomped through the service area with a red, angry face. Just like she'd never heard Mary yell, Bria had never seen Santos angry before and she didn't like it. She also didn't like the anguish on Mary's face as she followed after him.

"Santos," Mary called, but he pulled open the front door. "Santos!"

He hesitated for just a second over the threshold, but it was only for a second. Instead of turning around and smiling at her or pulling her into the bathroom to make out — while Bria and Charlie pretended not to know what they were doing — Santos stepped outside and slammed the door closed behind him.

Bria felt like he'd taken all the air from the room with him.

For a second, she was too nervous to move. Her gaze skittered left to right — Mary to Charlie — and then forward again. They watched in silence as Santos collected himself on the sidewalk in front of Confections. Bria was certain Santos would come to his senses and turn around, but then he stepped into the street and walked away without looking back. Bria's heart was pounding against her ribcage.

Charlie gasped lightly when Mary turned on her heels and stomped into the kitchen. She only made it a few steps before a low, pained wail fell from her lips. The sound was so heartbreaking, it jolted Bria into action. She spun around and rushed after her boss with Charlie hot on her heels. They found her in the kitchen with her face in her hands, tears leaking through her fingers.

Bria didn't know how to soothe her or fix this, so all they could do was hold her while she sobbed.

A small part of her wished she'd never left Sully's bed.

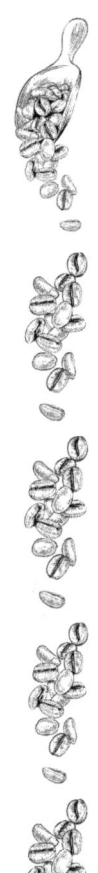

B ria was keeping Mary company in the kitchen while Charlie worked the storefront.

She sometimes got nervous when Mary watched her bake, even though she was always gentle in her corrections, but today Bria wished for her to chirp up and tell her she was overworking the dough or her chocolate was about to burn.

She wanted Mary to say anything so she didn't have to listen to more soft, sad sniffles from across the room.

It was Charlie's idea to call Lorraine. A perk of being nosy, apparently, was that Charlie was levelheaded in stressful situations — probably so she didn't miss a single detail while observing other people's drama. Either way, Bria was relieved the moment Lorraine swept into the kitchen.

With a teacake in hand.

"Where'd you get that?" Bria said.

Lorraine had half the cookie in her mouth and raised her eyebrows mid-bite. "Hmm?"

"I gave it to her," Charlie said, following her inside with two empty trays from the display case. "Compensation for helping us with..." She let the sentence trail off and nodded her head in Mary's direction.

"And I thank you for that," Lorraine said, dusting off her hands. "But I would've come for free." She said that after the cookie was long gone, only a small crumb in the corner of her mouth that she brushed away with an elegant tip of her finger.

Charlie smiled and shook her head, grabbing a rack of chocolate glaze donuts on her way back into the storefront.

"What happened?" Lorraine whispered.

Bria shook her head quickly and shrugged. Her tongue felt heavy at the thought of trying to explain what she'd seen but not knowing if she should, but then Mary sniffled pitifully again. Bria took a deep breath and forced herself to speak. "Santos," she started, and Mary barely swallowed another sad cry.

Bria licked her dry lips and started again, rushing

through this as fast as she could. "Santos stopped by earlier and they fought."

Lorraine squinted her eyes at her. "Who fought?"

"Santos," Bria said.

"With who?"

"Mary," Bria sighed.

"Who were they fighting?" Lorraine asked.

Bria rolled her eyes. "Each *other*."

"Oh my god," Lorraine gasped. She bent down in front of Mary and pulled her into a hug, whispering soft words while Mary started crying again.

Bria exhaled in relief before turning back to the dough to give them a little privacy. She was just about to dig her hands back in when she realized she *was* on the verge of over-working it. While Lorraine talked to Mary, Bria covered the dough with a clean towel and pushed it aside to rest.

The long night was starting to catch up to her, aided by the unexpected emotions after Santos and Mary's argument. It was a rare day when Bria wished for the end of her shift but today was definitely that day. She started cleaning up the prep table, daydreaming about crawling back into Sully's bed before her brain corrected it to her own. She had to bite the inside of her cheek not to smile at the thought while she worked, especially while Mary was still sniffling back her emotions.

She'd so thoroughly tuned out Mary and Lorraine — for their privacy — that when Lorraine popped up and called out, "We need a ladies' night," Bria actually jumped in surprise.

"Huh?" Her heart was pounding against her chest.

Lorraine was looking back and forth between her and

Mary. "We need to go out. Night on the town. Have a few drinks. Maybe dance a little."

Bria frowned. "In Sea Port?"

"Here?" Mary exclaimed.

"Yeah. Here. In Sea Port." She batted at the air and rolled her eyes. "Never mind. Meet me here in forty minutes." She squeezed Mary's shoulder and then turned toward the swinging door, swiping a chocolate chunk cookie from the tray.

"You're paying for that!" Bria yelled, but Lorraine was already through the door.

She pursed her lips and turned back to Mary. Her boss sniffled again and shrugged. "I'll add it to her tab," she whispered.

Bria was about to argue but Mary's eyes were still shimmering with tears, so she let that one cookie go.

For now.

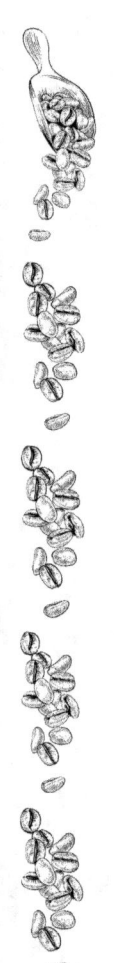

WELCOME TO SEA PORT

TWELVE

Ladies' Night Out

S ea Port sat right in the center of the driest county in
the South. Well, one of the driest.

Orange Grove County went dry during Prohibition and never looked back for reasons no one alive could
explain. Bria had asked. The ban on alcohol would've made
sense if the county was particularly religious or a hotbed of
illegal activity, neither of which had ever been true. Still, for
decades, Porties looking for a good — or even just okay —
bottle of liquor had been forced to drive just one county
over to find a liquor store which may or may not have even
been legal.

Bria knew a lot about Sea Port's history, but when
Lorraine led them deeper into one of Sea Port's older neighborhoods, she started to second-guess everything she
thought she knew. Downtown Sea Port wasn't really that
big, but a lot of the Transplants' lives hovered around those
few blocks that housed the town's few stores and even fewer
administrative buildings. But for *real* Porties, downtown

was just a pit stop they made their way through to get back to the heart of Sea Port, which lay in the land. The sidewalks only extended but so far before they gave out to dirt paths paved by foot traffic. Even the paved roads eventually gave way to packed dirt and then there was nothing but farmland as far as the eye could see.

Technically, there were five founding families in Sea Port — people who huddled together right at the end of the Civil War. People who wanted nothing more than to own the land they worked. They'd come together for safety more than anything else, but had tilled this land — which had been at least a quarter swamp back then — investing in a future they were almost too terrified to hope was close at hand. It was only after the war was well and truly done that they'd started to parcel out the land for each family. By then, there were nearly half a dozen families — or small huddles of people who were about the same — their freedom as new and tenuous as their town boundaries.

"Where are we going?" Bria hissed, trudging through the dry, grassy path as if she wasn't fucking exhausted. "Can't believe I just asked a Transplant that."

"Hey!" Mary and Lorraine said, spinning around to face her.

Bria stumbled back, her tennis shoes sinking into a patch of wet grass. "Sorry," she whispered, "but the rest of the question stands."

"Can't tell you yet," Lorraine said, twirling back around and stomping forward.

Mary winked at Bria before turning to follow. After sniffling all afternoon, Mary almost looked like herself again, and that was the only reason Bria kept her mouth shut and followed them even though she just wanted to sleep for the rest of the day.

"I think I deserve a raise," Bria called.

"These aren't business hours!" Lorraine yelled. "I don't want to talk any business."

"Good thing you're not my boss, then," Bria said, staring a hole into the back of Mary's head. Mary pretended not to have heard her and refused to even turn around. Bria pursed her lips and stepped around the old tree stump in their path — a tree stump that had been there all her life — without even thinking.

Old Ms. Kemp's white picket fence appeared in front of them and Lorraine's steps slowed. She reached over the fence to lift the latch.

"Don't do that," Bria called, channeling her own mother's warning. "Ms. Kemp collects shotguns."

Like most kids, Bria had spent her childhood riding her bike along this same road, running into everyone's yard — except Old Ms. Kemp's. Whenever the kids got too close to her fence, someone would yell out a warning and redirect them elsewhere. Bria just assumed she didn't like kids, which made sense, since she didn't seem to like anyone else anyway.

Lorraine was unfazed by her warning. "She also keeps a pistol in her purse," she shot back, popping the lock and opening the gate. Bria watched Lorraine step into Ms. Kemp's yard, her heart beating up into her throat.

"What the hell is going on?" Bria whispered.

"Let's see," Mary laughed.

"Oh, now you can hear me?"

"Make sure to close the gate," Lorraine whispered as loud as she dared.

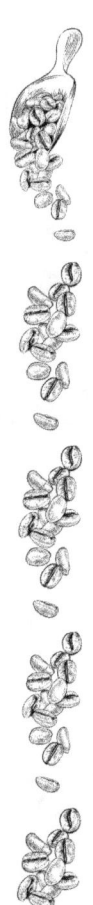

Bria stopped just outside the gate and looked behind herself as if her mother could appear out of thin air and drag her home by her ear, but there was no one there. No one to stop her but herself. She turned back to the gate and let her gaze move up the neat stone path to Ms. Kemp's wide wraparound porch. Bria never thought she'd step into this yard and the small girl inside her — the one who'd never be perceived as a fully grown adult to a quarter of the town's residents — was flashing warning lights in her brain. She wasn't supposed to be here; she was too young.

"Bria, come on," Mary called. She looked away from the stone path to find the other women halfway across the yard. She didn't want to be left behind, so she took in a deep breath, held it for the count of five, and then stepped into Ms. Kemp's front yard, exhaling loudly when the world didn't end.

She pushed the gate closed behind her, jumping at the sound of the metal latch connecting, and then followed a path she'd never seen before, rushing after Mary and Lorraine.

This stone path was just as neat as the one that led to the Kemp house but was sunken into the dirt and easy to miss with the naked eye, especially from the other side of the fence. The walkway narrowed as it rounded the house, forcing the women to walk in a line as they entered a wild forest of trees so thick they blocked out the sun.

"This is weird," Mary breathed.

"I know," Lorraine cried excitedly.

"Really weird," Bria whispered as they stepped into Ms. Kemp's backyard, which was not at all as she would've expected.

"Ta-da!" Lorraine exclaimed as they walked back into the sun.

Bria turned to Mary, who looked just as confused as she felt.

"Ta-da to what?" Mary asked.

Lorraine sucked her teeth and turned to Bria, her face bright and open, but she was just as clueless as Mary.

"Where the hell are we?" Bria asked.

"Wait, neither of you know?" Lorraine asked, shocked. "For real?"

"Know what, girl?" Mary asked.

"Wow," Lorraine breathed, smiling in triumph. "A Transplant gets to teach you something?"

Bria sucked her teeth. "Uncalled for."

Lorraine danced in place for a few seconds before stepping to the side with her arms spread out. "I am pleased to present to you Sea Port's only surviving speakeasy."

Mary gasped excitedly. "Oh my god, it's real?"

"The fuck is a speakeasy?" Bria asked.

The other women glared at her. "How old are you?" Mary shot back in an offended tone.

Bria rolled her eyes. "Don't pull that card. You've seen my ID."

"I haven't," Lorraine said, but then shrugged. "Speakeasies date back to Prohibition. They were bars where people could buy bootleg beer and listen to jazz."

"Ugh, imagine how good that music was," Mary sighed.

"Imagine how lethal that booze was," Lorraine laughed.

"Why the hell is there a speakeasy in Sea Port? Of all places! We're in the middle of nowhere."

Lorraine smiled. "That's exactly what I said when I came

across a reference to it in the diaries of... Never mind. Anyway, turns out Old Ms. Kemp is the great grand-daughter of a rum-running empire."

"Wait," Bria called, shaking her head. "You're telling me the Kemps were criminals, but not who mentioned the bar in their diaries?"

"Archives are complicated," Lorraine said with a shrug.

Bria rolled her eyes.

"Has it been here since Prohibition?" Mary asked.

"Just about. I think there was a fire in the Fifties, but they rebuilt it, obviously. They said it looks about the same as it did before, just a little bigger. Come on," Lorraine said.

"Wait," Bria called. They turned to her and it only made the fluttery anxiety in her stomach all the worse. "Do we need, like, an invitation or something?" she asked.

Lorraine shook her head. "Nah, the speakeasy is open to anyone who knows the password. Well, not quite *anyone*," she said, beckoning them to follow her.

"What's that mean?" Mary asked.

Lorraine walked across the grass toward a windowless wood wall. Bria had to tilt her head to the right and squint to see the outline of a door she wouldn't have noticed if Lorraine hadn't stopped right in front of it. Lorraine knocked on the distressed wood with three sharp raps and they waited in silence, breathing hard from their walk. The door squeaked open and a shadow of a figure appeared just outside of Bria's view. She squinted but still couldn't make out who was there.

"Password," the voice drawled. Bria didn't recognize that either.

"Shebeen," Lorraine whispered with an excited giggle.

Another few seconds of stillness passed before the shadowy figure disappeared and the door creaked slowly open. Lorraine beamed over her shoulder before waving for them to follow and plunging inside. Mary didn't hesitate to follow, but once again, Bria had to take a deep breath before she could do the same.

"Welcome to the Sea Port Ladies' Speakeasy," Mrs. Thornton said once they were cluttered into the hallway.

"Mrs. Thornton, what are you doing here?" Bria gasped, looking at her third-grade teacher with wide eyes.

"None of your business," the older woman sighed.

"Ladies?" Mary queried in a high-pitched tone.

"Yeah, ladies, in the classic sense. There's none of that soft women's lib, glass of wine shit here. We make our booze and throw it back just like the smart, strong, and industrious women who helped build this town did."

"Aw, I love that," Mary sighed happily.

"It's great, right?" Lorraine echoed.

"I don't remember nothing about this in the founder's play you directed," Bria said in a voice just on the boundary of disrespectful, but not over it. Mrs. Thornton had been the kind of teacher who used her wooden ruler for more than pointing at the board.

"You couldn't remember your *one* line in that play. Maybe you missed it," she shot back. "Go on in and get out of my hair."

"I'll keep track of them," Lorraine promised, leading Bria and Mary down a narrow, dark hallway.

"So," Lorraine whispered as they walked. "While I was looking in the *Sentinel* archives for any sign of this place, I ran into this one article about Old Ms. Kemp's aunt being arrested for running an illegal drinking establishment."

"Wow," Mary whispered.

"They called her Shebeen Sally, hence the password. I wasn't sure it was correct, so I came here to talk to Old Ms. Kemp and well, here we are. She said her aunt made the best bathtub gin she'd ever had. Premium hooch."

"Ew," Bria said.

"Hooch? Really?" Mary laughed.

Lorraine giggled with her. "I've been knee-deep in Sea Port archives from the Twenties for like a week. Leave me be. Anyway, Sally started bootlegging booze just for her friends at first, but then word got out that it was as good as the real thing — maybe even better — and she ramped up production. But transporting it across the county, even across town was risky, you know, because this place is the size of a pinprick. So she opened the speakeasy to ease distribution."

Mary was fully engrossed in the history lesson. "Wasn't that riskier?"

Lorraine led them into a wide room that looked like a mix between a bar and a library. Bria approved even through her confusion. There were low round tables and chairs dotted around the open space and they took the first table they came to. Lorraine's eyes were dancing with excitement.

"That's what I would've thought, but except for that one arrest, I can't find any evidence that Sally had any other problems. And clearly," she said, gesturing around her, "the speakeasy survived."

"But how? Why?" Mary asked eagerly.

"That's what I've been trying to find out. I've been trying to set up an interview with Old Ms. Kemp, this time on the record, but she's been dodging me. I've been meaning to come here with a little bit of backup, she can be a little intimidating."

"No shit," Bria muttered under her breath.

"I obviously couldn't bring Jonah, and you're usually... busy," Lorraine aimed at Mary, raising her eyebrows playfully.

Mary blushed just as a woman set three glasses onto the table.

"Oh, I don't—" Mary started.

"Mrs. Baxter!" Bria called, gaping up at her dance teacher from high school.

The woman sucked her teeth. "You old enough to be in here?" the older woman asked. She didn't even wait for an answer, though, shaking her head as she turned back to the bar. "I feel old as hell," she muttered to herself.

Bria reached for the glass and tipped it to her mouth. She thought about downing it, but sense and Lorraine's nervous cry came to her at the same time, so she took a small sip and felt like fire was burning a path down her tongue and throat.

"Oh, god," Bria gasped.

Mary reached for her, but Lorraine shrugged. "She'll be alright. Now, tell me exactly what the hell is going on with you and your men," she said, pinning Mary with her stare.

Bria's eyes were watering and she was starting to sweat, but she opened her ears completely. Charlie would never forgive her if she missed a single detail.

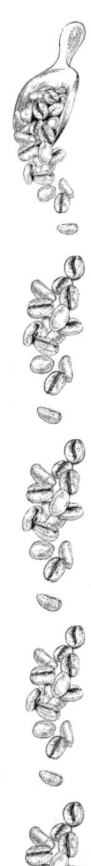

MARY

Mary lifted a glass to her lips and took what she thought was a small sip. Tiny, even.

"Dear god, what the fuck?" she spluttered out, coughing while the liquor burned her up from the inside out.

"See?" Bria wheezed.

While Mary tried not to cough up a lung, Lorraine sat back in her chair with a giddy smile. "Amateurs," she said to Mrs. Baxter.

The older woman hummed in disdain while she set three short glasses of water on the table. Lorraine pushed a glass each to Bria and Mary. Mary gulped down half the water and wiped at her warm forehead. A few tears fell from her eyes, but at least they weren't sad this time.

"Better?" Lorraine asked.

"What percentage alcohol is that?" Mary asked, wiping at her wet cheeks.

"Mmmm, best not to ask. Anyway, tell me what's going on? I want *all* the details," Lorraine pushed. She lifted her glass from the tabletop but stopped before it reached her lips. "Well, not *all* the details." She tilted her head to the side. "Some of them, though."

"Shut up," Mary chuckled.

Lorraine set her glass down and then leaned forward. Her smile softened and she set her hand on the table, reaching out for Mary without breaching her boundaries. "You three aren't breaking up, are you?"

Mary couldn't remember whose idea it was to call Lorraine, but she understood why they had. Her question was sincere and heartfelt, but not even in the realm of possibility. "Santos and Knox want to meet my family."

Lorraine sat up straight in her seat, let out a high-pitched squeal, and clutched her hands to her chest. Mary rolled her eyes and turned to look at Bria's unsurprised face.

"Charlie told me," Bria said, taking another tiny, baby, barely even a sip of her drink.

"Of course, she did," Mary said, shaking her head. "We were planning a road trip around Christmas to visit Santos's family in Denver and I was all for that. Then Knox wanted to take us to Vegas to meet a woman who's like his surrogate mother. It's gonna be so sweet," she said, smiling big enough to dislodge a couple more tears. "But then they started talking about visiting my family in Berkeley."

"Oh my god!"

"Are you going to keep doing that?"

"Yes!" she squealed again.

Mary rolled her eyes and took another sip of her water. She wasn't ready to try the hooch again yet.

"So, what's the problem?" Bria asked.

"Yeah. Do you think your family won't like them? Or that they'll be freaked out because your relationship is a little unconventional?"

"Who cares what my family thinks? Some of them might like them, some of them won't, but I don't care." Mary was trying to speak in a normal voice, but it seemed like every word that fell from her mouth was louder than the last. And

since the hooch had ripped her throat to shreds, it didn't feel great to find herself close to shouting, all in an effort to make herself sound surer than she felt. "How they feel doesn't matter and it won't affect my relationship."

Lorraine covered one of Mary's hands, which had balled into a fist while she was speaking without her knowing. "It's okay to be nervous about this," she whispered.

"I know," Mary cried, without tears this time. "*I* know, but Santos and Knox are very..." She was at a loss for words and just kind of shrugged sadly. "You've met them." Lorraine nodded and squeezed her hand. Mary took in a deep breath and let it out loudly. Painfully.

"I just know they're going to go there and try to be on their best behavior. They're gonna want to charm everyone, especially Knox." She pulled her hands away from Lorraine's and grabbed her drink. She took the smallest sip she could and then breathed through the burn, steeling herself to say the thing she couldn't tell the men she loved. "They're gonna want to make my entire family love them, and it'll crush them when they can't."

Lorraine nodded sympathetically. "Are you sure they can't charm everyone? Just show up and send Knox in, smile first." She fanned herself dramatically.

Mary couldn't help but smile even as her shoulders sagged. "It won't matter. My family is odd. We're not close. I'd already signed my lease for the bakery before I told my parents I didn't get tenure. I was on the road here before I told them about the move. And when I finally told them about the bakery, it was just a lot of...nothing."

"What do you mean, nothing?" Bria asked.

"I mean *nothing*. I texted them, they read the texts, and

no reply. Not for weeks. And when my mother finally *did* call, she just said, 'I guess it wasn't for you.'" Mary swiped a hot tear from her cheek.

"But it wasn't," Lorraine said softly. "You say so all the time."

"I know, but my mom told me in as many words that I couldn't hack it as an academic every year of graduate school. Even when I got that job, she just... I can't explain it, but it was like she thought I'd fail even then. So, when I didn't get tenure, all I could think was that she was right. That she'd always known I was a failure. I-I don't want Knox and Santos to have to deal with that. I don't want them to have to deal with her."

Lorraine stood from her chair and wrapped her arms around Mary's shoulders as she cried softly until she could compose herself. When she was better, Lorraine took her seat again, and all three women took small sips of their drinks.

"Is it gin?" Bria gasped. "And is it always this rough?"

"I wish I had the answers," Lorraine sighed before turning back to Mary. "Now don't shoot the messenger, but it sounds to me like maybe you do care if your family likes Knox and Santos."

Mary frowned but nodded. "And I hate that. I'm happier than I've ever been. I'm just...worried that if my mom doesn't like them, it'll all end."

Lorraine sat up straight and proper in her chair and smiled across the table at her. "As the local ambassador for adults with mom baggage," she started, and Mary chuckled softly, "it sounds to me like you're too worried to let your present and your past touch."

"Very."

"And it sounds like maybe you have a low self-esteem when it comes to dealing with your mother. Like maybe she's spent a lot of time undermining your confidence."

"A very long time."

Lorraine nodded. "Okay, well, as your closest girlfriend, geographically speaking, it's my place to say that you're literally one of the strongest, most confident people I've ever met. I can't even fathom you, Mary Woods, ever doubting yourself."

"You didn't know me before I came here," Mary mumbled.

"You're right. I didn't. The Mary who's afraid of letting herself be seen and wants to hide these men she loves away from the world is *not* the Mary who just debuted a ménage à truffle in her bakery."

Mary laughed through more tears.

"They're already a bestseller," Bria added gently, patting Mary's arm.

"Of course, they are!" Lorraine cried. "So maybe the Mary that I know is the one who should take this adorable ass road trip with her men."

"That's easier said than done," Mary sighed.

"Is it? What would be the biggest difference between this trip and the last time you went home?"

"I honestly can't even remember the last time I went home."

Lorraine sighed. "I realized as I was asking the question that it was a gamble. Anyway, I just meant that this time, you don't have to face your family alone. You have two big, strong, strapping—"

"No one says *strapping* anymore," Mary interjected.

Bria made a choking sound and sipped her water.

"Sorry, the Twenties. Anyway, you're with Santos and Knox and you three are a team. There's no need to face your family or anyone else alone anymore."

Mary chewed on the inside of her cheek for a minute as she mulled over Lorraine's words. "What you're saying makes sense," she admitted.

Lorraine beamed at them. "Jonah and I are really digging couple's therapy. It's been very illuminating."

"And it *might* be pretty similar to what Knox and Santos have been saying for days," Mary added.

"Well, then, there you have it," Lorraine said, knocking her fist against the table. She raised her hand and lifted her fingers one by one. "Knox, Santos, me, Jonah-by-proxy, and our couple's therapist all agree that you, Mary, are in a relationship with two partners and you should lean on them."

"One problem," Mary said, holding up her index finger. "What about Cat-leen?"

"We'll catsit her," Lorraine offered quickly, pursing her mouth as if that was obvious.

"And I'll watch the bakery," Bria said. "As the assistant manager."

Mary cut her eyes at Bria.

"Look at that. Everything's handled," Lorraine said happily.

Mary felt overwhelmed but in a good way, which was a great description of her life in Sea Port. She reached for her drink again, but another bony hand snatched it up before she could.

Mary shifted to see Old Ms. Kemp standing next to her

with a smirk on her face. "Oh, hi!" she said, squirming in her seat, but Ms. Kemp wasn't looking at her.

"You're back?" Ms. Kemp asked Lorraine in a dry voice.

"I am," Lorraine trilled back. "And I brought friends."

Mary beamed up at her, but it was Bria who caught Ms. Kemp's attention. "You ain't old enough to be in here. Are you?"

Bria sighed heavily. "Yes, Ms. Kemp. I've been old enough for a while. Does my mother know about this place?"

Ms. Kemp ignored Bria's question altogether to squint in Mary's direction. "Can you keep a secret, or do I need to worry about your little friends coming up here and putting their noses where they don't belong?"

Mary smiled innocently. It wasn't as dazzling as one of Knox's, but few things were. She held up her right hand as if she was taking an oath. "What Knox and Santos don't know won't hurt them."

Old Ms. Kemp considered her for a few seconds before nodding. "Alright. Now, are you ready for a real drink or you wanna keep sipping on this rotgut?"

Mary and Bria's mouths fell open. "You mean that's not the real hooch?" Bria cried.

Ms. Kemp rolled her eyes. "'Course it's not. If this is what we were selling, why the hell would half of Bolton County be coming over here for a drink?"

"Um, 'cause Bolton is dry too," Bria offered.

Ms. Kemp smirked. "Sure, it is," she said and turned away before calling at them over her shoulder. "Come on up to the bar when you're ready to order."

Mary turned her glare to Lorraine, who had a bright

smile on her face. "It's a little harmless hazing," she said, bouncing excitedly in her seat. "It's part of the experience."

"I think I'm done," Bria said, drinking the last of her water. She stood from her chair, wobbled a little bit, then took a deep breath, forcing a smile on her face. "I'll tell Knox and Santos you'll be out late."

"Thanks," Mary mumbled.

"Lightweight," Lorraine said in a reproachful whisper, but Bria was already stumbling toward the door. She hadn't had enough sleep or food to go on a bender in Old Ms. Kemp's backyard.

WELCOME TO SEA PORT

THIRTEEN

Sully

This day had not gone at all how she planned. Sully was a pretty easygoing person normally, but this day was pushing her to the limit. In the hours since Willie had dropped her bombshell, Sully felt like only half her brain was still in operation because nothing made sense.

Because how had she spent last night eating her best friend's little sister out?

Half-sister.

Sister.

"Come on," Willie called over her shoulder.

"Come on where?" Sully called back. "I thought we were getting a drink."

"We are," Willie said.

"Where? I have a whole bar at home."

Willie scoffed. "You have a cheap bar cart you inherited from that strange dude obsessed with frogs in our last apartment building and booze that's barely above well liquor."

Offended, Sully rolled her eyes at Willie's back. "You didn't say the *quality* of the drink," she muttered weakly.

Willie spared her the indignity of a response and they continued on their walk through Old Town Sea Port, as the newcomers called it. In reality, it was a neighborhood called The Grove, but not too many people called it that anymore. Even though Porties loved their history, Sully had realized that most people either couldn't remember the names of certain neighborhoods, buildings, and streets or they couldn't agree on the names they remembered. It was an odd little quirk she'd discovered after dozens of conversations with Porties of all ages, but it was charming as hell. The only reason Sully even knew this neighborhood had once been called The Grove was because of an old hand-drawn map hanging in Willie's office — a map that most people just glossed over, apparently.

She wondered if Bria knew and even just thinking her name made Sully's skin warm. Her hand moved to the outline of her cell phone in her back pocket, fingers itching to call Confections and hear Bria's voice. But Willie needed Sully, so she put her yearnings aside.

Well, she tried to. No matter how focused she was on Willie, she couldn't go more than a few moments before her thoughts drifted back to Bria. After a night spent drenched in the soft, lyrical rhythms of Bria's voice as she whispered and sighed, laughed and moaned, Sully couldn't wait to see her again, which made her feel guilty as hell even though she wasn't sure she had any reason to be.

At a white picket fence, Willie reached into the yard and unlatched the gate.

"So we're trespassing now?" Sully asked.

"Shh," Willie hissed. "Shut the gate closed behind you."

Sully exhaled far louder than necessary and followed Willie to a wide, perfectly manicured lawn. She pulled the gate closed gently and then carefully made her way down a dirt path, around the big house with red shutters, into a dense little collection of trees. The sun was low in the sky when they finally left Willie's office, but once they stepped under the trees, it was dark as dusk.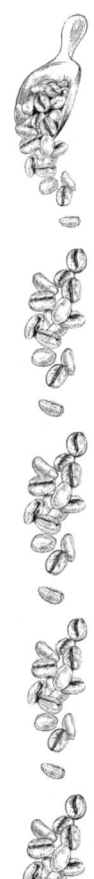

"I'm not getting arrested for you again," Sully whispered.

"Why are you whispering?" Willie shot back. "And you were in that bar fight with me."

"Because of you. Words mean things," Sully hissed. "Are you going to answer my question?"

Willie stopped and turned toward her. Her face was hidden in shadow, but Sully could feel her best friend's eyes on her. "Are you going to answer *mine*?"

Sully crossed her arms and smirked at her friend. "It's really nice to know that even in the midst of your existential crisis, you're still a pain-in-the-ass politician."

Willie stepped forward and a ray of light made its way through the treetops, giving Sully a full view of her mocking grin. Even though Sully and Willie had instantly clicked, their relationship had always been full of bickering; arguing was their love language. So when Willie smirked at her but didn't open her mouth to speak, she knew her friend wasn't doing great. No, that was an understatement. When Sully looked at the soft curves of Willie's face, all she could see was pain.

"Where are we going, Will?" Sully asked in her softest, gentlest voice.

When Willie blinked, Sully thought she saw a slight watery sheen in her eyes, but it was gone in an instant.

"Old Ms. Kemp has a speakeasy in her cellar," Willie finally answered. "Best hooch in Sea Port," she said as she walked deeper into the thicket of trees.

"Who the fuck calls it hooch?" Sully whispered. "And why is this town so fucking weird?"

WILLIE

On Willie's eighteenth birthday, her mother brought her to Old Ms. Kemp's cellar for one drink. Just one. It was a rite of passage on her mom's side to mark a young woman's passage into independence with a glass of Old Ms. Kemp's booze. It wasn't a Waltham tradition, which had annoyed her father because he couldn't tag along — not just because he was a man but as Mayor, he couldn't openly admit to knowing the cellar even existed. Apparently, the Waltham men had their own ritual, but Willie was — had thought she was — her father's only child, so what did she know or care about what the Waltham men did?

Willie didn't know much about the Stone family, but she found herself wondering how Bria had marked her own transition into adulthood. Following the train of those thoughts made her stomach tie itself into a new knot she desperately wanted to drink away.

"You here in your official capacity?" Loretta Thornton asked at the door.

"No, ma'am," Willie sighed, wishing they didn't interrogate her every time she stopped by. She stood still as Mrs. Thornton looked her over before turning her critical gaze on Sully. After a frustratingly long inspection, Loretta waved both women inside and shut the door behind them.

"Follow me," Willie said.

They stepped into a small pantry Old Ms. Kemp used mostly as a front. It had been decades since the speakeasy had been raided, but the pantry stood as a thin line of defense just in case someone — not Willie — wanted to make a fuss. Through the pantry, they walked down a short, narrow hallway that opened up into the familiar barroom Willie had come to know and love. Unfortunately, the comfort she felt was instantly dashed when she spotted Mary and Lorraine standing at the bar, talking to Ms. Kemp.

Since she'd become the mayor, the cellar was one of the only places in town where Willie could find some peace. It was usually full of women her mother's age or older, women who refused to treat her like anything more than the tall, chatty little girl with too many opinions. Some days, they made her life a living hell, but she'd take that over the blind support some of the Transplants gave her. They only knew her as Mayor Waltham, and some of them never seemed ready for her to be just herself, so once she saw Mary and Lorraine, she seriously considered turning around and leaving.

If only there were other bars in town. This singular moment convinced Willie to make repealing that damn Prohibition-era law the center of her reelection campaign.

She was still thinking about running when Old Ms. Kemp spotted her. "Well, hello there, Mayor. What can I get you?"

Mary and Lorraine smiled in her direction. She smiled back as professionally as she could muster. "Bourbon," Willie said. "*Two*."

"You always did take after your father," Old Ms. Kemp said, shaking her head.

Those words shook her to her core and it was only Willie's poise — only an entire lifetime of being her father's daughter — that kept her standing when she wanted to fall to her knees.

"Actually, make mine a gin," Willie said, walking to the bar. "My mama says it's better than anything I can buy."

Mary and Lorraine moved farther down the gleaming wooden bar. Legend had it Old Ms. Kemp's great-great-uncle cut it from the first oak on this land, but Willie knew that was as likely to be a fairy tale as the truth.

"That's 'cause your mama's got taste," Ms. Kemp said with a dry chuckle. Her hand had stilled over a bottle of amber liquid with a slightly off-center handwritten label pasted across the front. "What about you, Ms. Sullivan? You wanna try my gin too?"

"Uh, yeah, sure," Sully said. "Hey, Mary. Hey, Lorraine."

"Hi, Sully," Mary called down the bar teasingly.

Lorraine smiled in their direction but her attention was focused squarely on Ms. Kemp. "So was the recipe your grandmother's...?"

Ms. Kemp sighed in reply. Willie watched Ms. Kemp pour their drinks only because she couldn't look in Mary's direction. Willie liked Mary and Lorraine, but it was hard to look at them and not see Bria. Even worse, now it was hard to look at Sully without seeing her too. She was still wrapping her head around the fact that she had a sister; she wasn't nearly ready to think too hard about the fact that her best friend had spent the night with her.

She was grateful when Ms. Kemp put two shot glasses in front of them. Willie reached for one, but Ms. Kemp swatted her hand away. "That'll be ten dollars," she said. "Cash only."

Willie pursed her lips while reaching into her purse. "You know bars in big cities let people open tabs."

"Good for them," the older woman replied.

Willie pulled a twenty-dollar bill from her wallet and slid it across the bar. "For the next round," she said.

"Gotcha," Ms. Kemp replied as Sully snatched one of the shot glasses.

Willie and Sully turned to one another, tapped the glasses together, and tipped them into their mouths. For a brief second, it was like old times.

They set their glasses back on the bar and Ms. Kemp was ready with the bottle. "So, was she right?" she asked.

"She usually is," Willie gasped. "Don't tell her I said that."

They grabbed their drinks and walked to an empty table, far enough away from Mary and Lorraine that they could speak in private.

"Let's pace ourselves, yeah?" Sully said with a gentle smile. "We're not in college anymore."

The bark of laughter that left Willie's mouth was harsh. Bitter. "We sure aren't," she whispered back. "We're real adults. I'm the Mayor. And you're dating my..." — she

lowered her voice again — "sister." She'd only just managed to stop her brain from tripping over that word, but her tongue was still unaccustomed. In fact, today was the first time she'd ever said the word aloud, and she still didn't know how to feel about it — the word or the person.

"How'd you find out?" Sully asked.

Willie took a small sip of her gin. Now that she wasn't shooting it down, she could appreciate it for more than the fact that it didn't burn her throat to shreds. She licked her lips and shifted uncomfortably in her seat.

"I was pulling information on the Waltham family exhibit for next year's Founder's Day celebrations. Lorraine wanted the family's descendants to put together something small for the library and since I'm... Since I thought I was the last Waltham, I wanted to use some artifacts we don't normally share. I was gonna loan our Bible to the library, since it's been in the family since they settled here and it has all of my great aunt Amy's scribbles."

"Sweet," Sully breathed.

"It also has the family tree inside. They started recording it in the Civil War, but they went back three generations in slavery, recording what they could remember. I've always loved that book and I thought it might be nice to share." Willie blinked rapidly, trying to stop the tears building in her eyes from falling.

"And Bria's in the Bible?" Sully asked carefully, leaning close to make sure not to be overheard.

Willie nodded.

"But...how? Who put her name there? Your father?"

Willie brought the shot glass to her mouth and drained

it as a fresh wave of tears started falling. "Nope. It wasn't his handwriting."

"Then maybe it's not true," Sully nudged. "Maybe it was a prank or mistake or something?"

Sully was throwing any and everything at the wall, trying to find some way around this truth. It didn't change anything, but she appreciated the effort, nonetheless.

"No need. I already know who wrote her name in the Waltham Bible. I recognized the handwriting." She grabbed Sully's shot glass and tipped the clear liquid into her mouth. Her throat had numbed now and the liquor floated down easy as lukewarm water. She licked gin from her lips and met Sully's eyes. "It was my mother."

"Holy shit!" Sully yelled.

Old Ms. Kemp laughed. "I told ya. Ain't nothing like my grandmother's gin."

"So it *is* your grandmother's recipe!" Lorraine yelled from across the room.

SULLY

Sully wasn't drunk-drunk, but she wasn't sober either. She'd spent a lot of strange nights at random bars with Willie over the years, but this had to be in the top ten. Maybe even top five. There was just so much going on.

After her confession, Willie had practically shut down,

only opening her mouth for more gin. She used to be the life of the party, the girl who could walk into a dead dive bar and bring it to life in two shots and half a pint. Willie was social lubrication in human form. She looked nothing like that girl tonight as she pretended to listen to another one of Ms. Kemp's stories.

"Now let me tell you young'ns what The Grove used to be like." She had a thin, unlit cigar dangling from the corner of her mouth, bobbing with every word, a glass of whisky on the table beside her, and a pair of readers precariously perched on the tip of her nose. "Back in my day," she started but was interrupted by Mary and Lorraine's giggles. Ms. Kemp didn't enjoy being interrupted and raised her eyes over the low rim of her glasses, fixing them in her stare.

Mary took a deep sip of her drink and Lorraine mouthed the word "sorry" before Ms. Kemp got back to her story.

Sully watched the exchange as further confirmation of just how not drunk she was. She turned to Willie to see if she had anything to say about them, but Willie was downing another shot. When she tipped her head back, a tear fell from the corner of her eye.

The saddest thing Sully had ever seen.

"We used to have these dances in the summer when it was too hot to even think," Old Ms. Kemp started before Sully tuned her out with a soft sigh.

She pulled her cell phone from her pocket and found Bria's number. All morning, she'd been trying to think of a cute first text to her, but the one she actually had to type out had not been on the list.

> I really wanted to see you tonight, but I don't think I can. Willie needs me.

She stared at the text for a few seconds, scrutinizing every word just in case she somehow betrayed Willie's secret.

Bria texted back almost immediately.

> Damn! I had plans for you.

Sully read Bria's message and felt on the verge of tears herself. She reached for her shot glass only to have Willie snatch it from her fingers before she could drink it.

"Bitch," Sully muttered.

"That's what he said," Mary giggled, and Lorraine joined in.

Ms. Baxter appeared out of nowhere to refill their glasses. While Willie was sliding her another ten-dollar bill, Sully snatched her glass and tipped half of it into her mouth before going back to Bria's message.

There were hundreds, maybe even thousands of things she could text back. Unfortunately, all her favorite retorts were unsuitable for public, so she played it safe.

> Plans can be rescheduled! If she wasn't my best friend, I'd leave her here. I swear!

Sully pressed send and then glared over the top of her phone at Willie, but her sour mood evaporated at Willie roughly wiping her wet cheek.

"So, next thing you know, everybody's got a damn pistol!" Old Ms. Kemp cried.

Sully's phone vibrated with another message from Bria.

> Nice to know you'd dip out on acquaintances for me.
>
> And plans can definitely be moved. Whenever you're ready, I will be too.

Sully's heart started racing and she set her shot glass back on the table, willing to sacrifice it to Willie's greedy, drunken grasp.

> I'm ready

Sully's message sent just as Bria's came in.

> I'm ready now 😊

"Fuck," Sully muttered to herself.

"Shh," Mary and Lorraine hissed.

Sully cut her eyes at the other women before shifting her focus back to her phone. Her fingers hovered over the screen as she tried to think of something suitably sexy to say, but it was hard to think straight with Willie sulking beside her and all the hooch.

So she opted for heartfelt over horny.

> Last night was one of the best of my life. I can't wait to see you again.

It was true, but words couldn't fully convey exactly how

strongly she felt and she was nervous to make an admission after just one date, but Bria's reply made her smile.

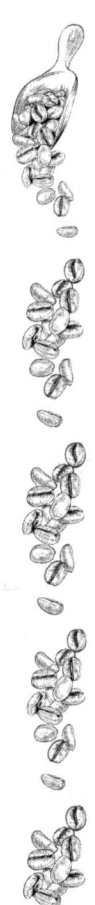

"Oh, somebody's got a somebody," Mrs. Thornton called from behind the bar. "What's his name?"

"It's Bria," Mary blurted out and then slapped a hand over her mouth.

Sully's eyes shifted to Willie. For the first time in what felt like hours, her best friend was looking at her with eyes glassy from unshed tears.

"This is the weirdest night of my life," she muttered to herself as a guilt she didn't even understand washed over her.

"The weird nights are the good ones," Ms. Kemp said. "Now drink up. Last round."

"What? No!" Mary cried very drunkenly.

"Thank god," Sully whispered.

WELCOME TO SEA PORT

FOURTEEN

Santos

Sea Port was so small there was almost no need for the police to have a regular night shift. Most businesses shut down at dusk and traffic all but stopped at about the same time. The only real traffic after dark were Porties on an evening walk to visit with one another or to settle their food before bedtime. Santos left the office at about nine and if anyone in town needed anything, they just called him at home.

There were only about four days a year when Santos and the rest of Sea Port's tiny police force ever had to work past ten — New Year's Eve, Founder's Day for the Founder's Day parade, Juneteenth for the Emancipation parade, and Christmas Eve for the...you guessed it, pageant and parade. Porties loved a good parade and Santos, at the very least, appreciated the consistency.

But he'd been in Sea Port long enough to know not to get too comfortable. So, even though he hadn't planned to see about a noise disturbance in Old Grove, he wasn't that shocked he was there. Or that Knox had tagged along.

"You wanna talk about what happened?"

"Nothing happened," Santos lied.

"Not what I heard."

Santos didn't dignify that fishing expedition with a response. He already felt bad enough; he didn't want to drag Knox down with him. Besides, the only person who could tell Knox about how pissed-off Santos had been and how horribly he acted was Mary, and she'd been radio silent for hours, so Knox didn't know everything yet.

"I won't judge," Knox said, interrupting Santos's brooding.

"Yeah, you will."

"So there's something to judge?" Knox asked.

There were only two stop signs in Sea Port and Santos blew through one of them. There were hardly any cars out anyway.

"Did—" Knox started, but Santos cut him off.

"Keep a lookout, Sergeant."

Of course, Knox didn't take kindly to what sounded like a command. Santos watched his shadowed figure turn toward him in the passenger seat. "That an order?" Knox asked.

Santos licked his lips. The words were right on his tongue, words that would annoy and arouse Knox in just a few syllables, but his heart wasn't in it. Knox lifted his left hand to the back of Santos's neck. His strong fingers massaged muscles so tight that first touch hurt.

"Thought so. Nothing's as bad as it seems," Knox whispered.

"It could be," Santos said, giving some voice to the fear he'd been living with since he'd stormed out of Confections. "You weren't there. I could've fucked it all up for all you know."

Knox's laughter rumbled through the car as his fingers slipped into the neck of Santos's sweatshirt. Santos blinked slowly, trying to focus on the dark country road. "If Mary didn't leave when you tried that no-sugar diet, I don't think she's gonna leave now."

Santos wanted to hear that, but that's why he couldn't believe what Knox said. He had this preternatural ability to just know what other people needed and give it to them. It's why

Santos and Mary were never mad at him. How could they be? And how could he be mad at Mary? These questions were why Santos sometimes worried that if this all fell apart, it would be on his shoulders. It would be his fault.

He was just about to say those words — or something close — when he spotted dark figures on Old Ms. Kemp's lawn.

"Is that the Mayor?" Santos asked, turning on his high beams.

Knox's fingers stopped moving. They both squinted through the windshield and then Knox laughed. "And there's our girl."

Santos sighed loudly, easing to a stop in the middle of the street. Knox unbuckled his seat belt and climbed out. Santos turned down his headlights and put the car in park. He let Knox take the lead, even though it made him feel like a coward.

"Babe! And babe!" Mary yelled.

"You drunk?" Knox laughed.

"Very," Sully said. "They all are."

"Rude," Lorraine slurred.

Mayor Waltham didn't speak; she was too busy shaking the gate. "Why won't it open?" she cried, sounding on the verge of tears.

Sully sighed before moving around Lorraine to lift the latch. "Very drunk," she said again.

Willie tripped out of Ms. Kemp's yard but Sully caught her. Lorraine and Mary were laughing and leaning on one another as they stumbled behind them.

Knox rushed to Mary and she fell into his arms. Jealousy ran hot through Santos's veins, so he shifted his attention to the other women and did his job. "We got a call about a noise disturbance," he said, eyes focused on the Mayor.

"Not us," Sully said.

"Nope!" Lorraine yelled. Mary's loud cackle joined the symphony.

"Sure," Santos breathed in a bored tone.

"What are you all doing out here?" Knox asked.

"Visiting a friend," Mayor Waltham said quickly, sounding almost sober.

Santos squinted in her direction. "And who exactly was that?"

"Not y'all bringing the cops to my door," Old Ms. Kemp called.

Her porchlight flickered on and illuminated the messy scene in front of them. Mayor Waltham's eyes were glassy. Sully was shaking her head softly. Meanwhile, Lorraine was leaning on Mary, who was leaning on Knox.

"Are the night calls always this eventful?" Knox asked around a laugh.

"No," Santos ground out. "Good evening, Ms. Kemp."

"Copper," she replied. Lorraine, Mary, *and* Knox burst into giggles.

"Can you tell me what's going on here?"

"Nope. Y'all have a good night," she said, pulling her gate closed and starting back up the path to her home.

"Of course," Santos muttered to himself.

"Are you two still mad at me?" Mary asked in a small voice.

Santos turned sharply in her direction. Her arms were wrapped around Knox's waist, her cheek pressed to his chest, but she was looking at Santos with big, sad brown eyes. He felt infinitely worse than just a few minutes ago.

Santos was on the job, but he forgot about everything and everyone that wasn't Mary or Knox. He moved to her side and leaned down to meet her eyes. "I was never mad at you," he said carefully. "Just frustrated. We can fix frustrated."

"We sure can," Knox said, kissing the top of Mary's head.

"Can we fix it in bed?" Mary whispered, brushing her fingers through Santos's beard.

"That's my girl," Lorraine whispered.

"Alright, we're out of here," Sully called.

Santos winked at Mary before standing straight. "Wait, we'll get you all home."

"How?" Sully asked, nodding her head toward his squad car.

Santos exhaled loudly. "Alright, maybe—"

"We'll walk," Mayor Waltham said.

"No," Santos and Knox barked at the same time.

Sully clearly didn't like that.

"Okay, look, how about I send Knox home with Mary and Lorraine and I'll walk you two back to your house?"

Mayor Waltham exhaled loudly. "Not to be rude, Chief Santos, but I've been walking these streets at night longer than you've been in Sea Port. Far longer."

While true, Santos couldn't hear anything besides the soft slur underneath her words. "How many times have you done it drunk?" he asked.

"Well, actually—" Willie started, but Sully cut her off.

"I'm not drunk. I only had a couple shots and lots of water. I'll get us home and I'll text when we make it."

Santos shook his head, but Sully kept going. "We only live five minutes from here," she said. "We aren't all out there on the outskirts of town like you."

Mary and Lorraine whispered something to one another before dissolving into more giggles.

He wanted to say no, but Mayor Waltham was stubborn. When he glanced at her, she was swaying a little bit but glaring at him, readying herself for a fight. He knew her well enough to know that she'd argue just to argue and it would take the same time as her walk home. He didn't like it, but if today taught him nothing, it was that he needed to learn which battles to fight and which ones to let go.

He shifted his gaze to Sully. "Text me literally as soon as you get home."

"Aye aye, captain," Sully said. Mary and Lorraine's giggles got louder.

"How drunk are you?" Knox asked as he steered them toward Santos's car.

"Very," Mary sighed.

"Ms. Kemp's grandmother's recipe is legendary. And maybe not in the best way," Lorraine sighed.

"What's that mean?" Knox asked.

"Nothing!" Mary said quickly. "Don't listen to her, she's drunk."

Santos sighed loudly and made eye contact with Sully again. She grabbed Mayor Waltham's hand and started leading her down the street. "As soon as you get home," he called after them.

"Yeah, yeah," Sully replied, waving goodbye without turning around.

Santos helped Knox get Mary and Lorraine in the back seat as the other women walked away.

"I love you," Mary slurred as he leaned over to buckle her seat belt.

Santos cupped her cheeks and brushed his mouth over hers. She smelled like sugar and booze. "I love you too. Even if you're drunk as hell."

"Good," she said and then hiccuped.

Knox's laughter filled the car as Santos drove them home.

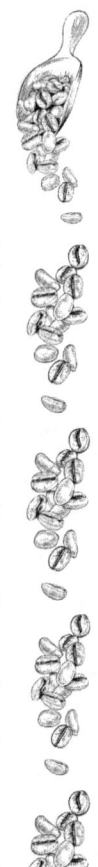

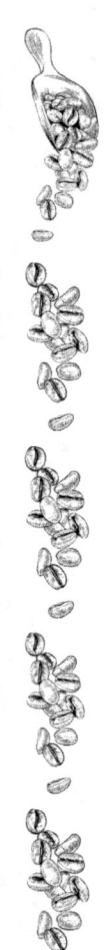

WELCOME TO SEA PORT

FIFTEEN

Willie

Willie blinked into consciousness with a drum set pounding against her temple like a Florence and the Machine breakdown. Her back hurt, her stomach felt like a boat on rocky seas, and her neck was stiff from sleeping wrong. It was official: Willie Waltham was too damn old for a hangover.

It took at least half an hour and too much effort to crawl out from under her comforter and then she had to shuffle toward the door, which was a fight all by itself. She took a quick break against the doorjamb to catch her breath. She'd had a lot of embarrassing hangovers, but this one was shaping up to be the worst if only because she hadn't had that much to drink last night. She had to stop a couple more times on the way to the bathroom and felt like she'd gone for a 5k run by the time she made it.

Willie used to love lazy mornings — tea and breakfast in bed, sharing the newspaper until it was time to strip the sheets and shower — but she hadn't had a day like that since she moved back home. She climbed into the shower feeling like a dried-out corn husk even though she had a vague memory of Sully forcing her to drink water before bed — although that could've been a memory from last night or a decade ago. She turned on the shower and jumped when the ice-cold water hit her skin, not moving until the water was comfortably hot and she felt awake and alive — a hangover trick that never let her down.

She couldn't remember her schedule. She didn't even know what time it was, so she accepted the fact that she was probably missing a meeting right now, but she didn't have the energy to move any faster so she didn't try.

"I'm never drinking again," she groaned loudly.

If it were at all possible to wash away all the gin she drank last night, she would've — she certainly tried — but she still had to hold onto the towel rack as she climbed from the tub. She felt almost human again, so that was a win — still a little achy and with a mouth drier than the Sonoran Desert, but human. She wrapped herself in her fluffiest towel and made a detour downstairs for ice-cold water and an electrolyte package before she really started her day.

In her bedroom, Willie found her cell phone plugged in and waiting on the nightstand, with a sticky note stuck to the screen covered in Sully's familiar block letter hand-writing.

NO MORE GIN!
CALL ME. LOVE YOU.

Willie pulled the note from her phone and pressed it

against her chest. "She's never gonna let me live this down," she sighed in soft resignation.

She hid her turmoil at the time, but the decision to move home hadn't come easy. She left Sea Port to see more of the world and she had, but that life had only lasted a few years. There were countries she still wanted to visit, new people she still wanted to meet, and most of all, there were memories of the life she'd been living that haunted her to this day. Independence had only lasted a short time, but it clung to her like a second skin, even in tiny little Sea Port.

If Sully hadn't uprooted her entire life to move with her, Willie didn't think she would've survived her homecoming. She loved Sea Port, but she missed her old life every day. More than anyone, Willie owed her friend for helping her stay grounded in the person she'd become, not just the person Porties expected her to be. She also owed Sully for getting her home safe and sound last night.

She stuck the sticky note to her lamp and opened her phone to check her calendar, surprised to find that her morning was mercifully light. Not light enough to get back into bed, but light enough that she didn't have to make any phone calls or email any apologies — but only if she was out of the house ASAP.

Willie's closet was separated by the lives she lived. The clothes on the left were bold and full of colorful prints and statement pieces. She'd carefully crafted her aesthetic the second she left Sea Port, honing her sartorial expression to perfection. The right was less exciting, a lot of monochromatic black with pops of red and a deep earthy bronze for a little variety; colors that conveyed strength and maturity to her constituents, especially the ones who remembered her in beads and knockers. The longer she'd been back in Sea Port, the less time she got to spend on the left side of her closet, and every day she missed that version of herself something fierce.

Instead of grabbing the first black dress she saw, Willie moved to the left, pushing hangers aside until she could reach all the way to the back of her closet. Her stomach started twisting again when her fingers rested on a familiar, hidden plastic garment bag. She remembered this sweater with crystal clarity — the way it looked, the way it felt against her cheek, and the man whose warm scent was embedded in every fiber. The urge to move the plastic aside and rub her cheek against the soft wool was so strong her fingers itched with need, but it had been almost eight years since he'd last worn it and every year his scent faded. She'd been preparing herself for the day she pulled that zipper open and smelled nothing. She wondered if her heart would ache less when that happened or more. Or if it would even matter by then.

That garment bag was a reminder of the life Willie could have lived. A life with a beautiful man who deserved better than someone who never really had two feet in his world.

Willie grieved her father in the exceptional moments: his birthday, her birthday, the first baseball game of the season — days she would have shared with him — but she missed Danny on regular mornings like this. Mornings when he would've pushed her to clear her calendar so they could drink tea and eat bacon sandwiches in bed. Willie missed Danny when Mary debuted a new pastry at Confections.

Willie missed Danny with every breath.

Her mother said people grieved at the same rate they

loved, meaning she loved Danny with her entire self, but that wasn't enough to grieve their relationship.

She assumed her mother had a sweater at the back of her closet that still smelled like Willie's father, but considering her latest revelations, she wasn't too sure anymore. Her mother had been the perfect picture of widowhood ever since his homegoing ceremony, but whatever her mother felt in the privacy of her home, she didn't share that with Willie or the town. Even in widowhood, Celia Waltham was the consummate politician's wife; an even more astute politician than Willie or her father could ever hope to be.

When the first tear hit the garment bag, Willie used her towel to dry her face and carefully put the sweater back on the rod. She was hungover and breaking her own heart; a terrible way to start the day.

She grabbed the first outfit she saw — a charcoal black power suit — snatched a lavender tank top from the dresser, and got dressed in record speed. She was Willie Waltham, daughter of Skip and Celia Waltham, the latest in a long line of Sea Port Walthams, and she had a job to do, hangovers and heartbreaks be damned.

When she was dressed and felt almost put together, she headed to the kitchen to rustle something up for breakfast but froze at the bottom of the stairs. Sully was sitting at the small table Willie barely used looking uncomfortable as hell, but it was the other woman that made her chest feel painfully tight.

"Mama?" Willie whispered in a shaky voice.

Her mother's face was a beautiful mask. "I hear you found your Great Aunt Amy's Bible," Celia said in that regal voice Willie knew all too well. This was the voice she used

when they left Sea Port — with people she worried would judge her accent. This was the voice her mother used when she thought she needed to protect herself. Willie sometimes mimicked her when she was giving a speech, but on her tongue, it always sounded the way Willie felt right now, like a little girl prancing around the house in her mother's high heels.

Willie nodded and swallowed a sudden lump of fear in her throat.

Celia inhaled loudly and exhaled through her mouth. "Sit down, little girl. I think it's time we talked."

WELCOME TO SEA PORT

SIXTEEN

Bria

Bria woke up in her own bed with the slightest hangover, which was exactly why she left Old Ms. Kemp's speakeasy after one glass of that damn rotgut. She was a lightweight, but she also knew her limits, and whatever the hell they were brewing up in that bar was out of her league. Besides, one look at sad Mary and Bria knew she'd have to open Confections today. They couldn't both be hungover. Someone had to be sober enough to temper chocolate, especially since Bria didn't know exactly what kind of health insurance they had to cover serious injuries. She'd find out when she was assistant manager, but until then, better safe than sorry.

Bria slept with her cell phone under her pillow, so she fished it out, hoping for something she'd never let herself say aloud just in case, but she smiled giddily when she saw exactly what she wanted. She flopped onto her back and kicked her feet while she unlocked her phone to read Sully's text message.

> You have no idea how much I missed you tonight.

She was beaming while she responded.

> I missed you too!

She'd had the house to herself last night and took advantage of the early morning privacy in the only way she could imagine — by masturbating to memories of her night with Sully. She would've preferred to skip across town to Sully's house for the real thing, but since that was off the table, she replayed their date with her hand in her panties until she fell asleep. Not a bad night, but it could've been better.

Sully didn't reply immediately. She might not have even been awake, but Bria was too impatient to wait, so she double texted.

> Busy day?

Bria was trying to sound nonchalant, but she held her breath until Sully finally replied.

> Very. You?

> Yeah. I need to get to the bakery in a few. But I'm not too busy to see you again. If you have time.

Bria chewed on her bottom lip for a few seconds before deciding to clarify.

> If you wanted to see me, obviously. If not, that's okay.

The chat bubble of Sully's response popped up immediately and she watched it, waiting with bated breath, but the longer it took, the more worried she became. Worried that the answer would be no, but then the bubble disappeared completely and that felt even worse.

She checked the time at the top of her phone screen, frowning as she climbed out of bed. She took a quick, hot shower, then pulled on a pair of leggings and an oversized t-shirt — the closest Confections came to a uniform — all the while keeping an eye on her phone, but Sully's reply never came. She walked to work with both eyes on her phone since she knew the route like the back of her hand. Sully still hadn't responded by the time Bria let herself into the back of the bakery and that had her in a bad mood.

The only good thing about this disappointment coming first thing in the morning was that Bria had the entire kitchen and storefront to herself. She let Stevie Wonder and cookie dough take her mind off Sully's silence. What else could she do?

Once her hands were washed and her apron was tied tight, Bria moved to the bakery's fridge to study the dough schedule. Usually, she and Mary planned their baking together at the end of a shift, but for obvious reasons they'd skipped that yesterday. She thought about calling Mary just to confirm, but then she remembered Mary's holiday road trip. All the visit to Old Ms. Kemp's had clarified for Bria was that Mary would be making up with Santos and Knox and they'd be gone over the holidays,

which would be Bria's time to shine. Sure, Mary had been too emotional to agree to Bria stepping in as the assistant manager, which meant Bria needed to take every opportunity to show her boss that she was the right person for the job. Mary had a five-year plan for the bakery, and so did Bria. Moving from Mary's assistant to assistant manager to Mary's business partner wouldn't be easy, but Bria was ready to put in the work. Her cookie-shaped goals couldn't be derailed, so whenever Mary showed up today, Bria wanted her to walk into a kitchen running like a well-oiled machine.

Bria only glanced at her phone once before she threw herself into work. Every day they needed teacakes, donuts, and muffins, so she started there. They kept meticulous track of every crumb that went into the display cases or left the kitchen already boxed for transport to other businesses and private homes around town. The only person who knew this list more intimately than Mary was Bria, and she reminded herself of that while she started weighing and sifting flour. By the time she'd started mixing a small batch of bagels, she felt at ease in a way she only could in Confections. The bagels made her think of Sully, but she shoved that urge down and stayed the course, trying not to let her mood flag again.

Bria was beating egg whites in the stand mixer, waiting for stiff peaks when her music abruptly shut off. For a second, she thought it was a phone call, maybe from Sully, but then Charlie walked into the kitchen with a smirk on her face.

"Morning."

"What are you doing here so early?" Bria asked.

Charlie gasped in faux shock. "Is that any way to greet your coworker?"

"Sorry. I'm not feeling great."

"Oh! Did you see our coffee-flavored friend again last night?"

"She's *not* coffee-flavored," Bria cried out.

"You'd know," she mumbled, dropping her backpack in the office.

"Why are you here?" Bria asked, trying to stop the shocked laughter she felt bubbling in her chest from bursting past her lips.

"'Cause this is a place of business and I'm on the schedule. Obviously," Charlie said, rolling her eyes. "Also, after yesterday, I thought you might need help with the opening shift."

That sounded all well and good, but Bria had known Charlie her entire life and nothing was ever that simple with her. She checked the clock on the wall. "We don't open for another forty minutes and you don't like doing kitchen work. What am I missing?"

Charlie beamed as she moved to the handwashing station. "Because there's so much news and I need someone to share it with."

Bria rolled her eyes and turned back to her egg whites. "Not interested."

Charlie's shoes squeaked against the floor and she appeared at Bria's side, drying her hands on a paper towel. "You sure about that? Because apparently, your new girlfriend was in the thick of it."

Bria stopped the mixer just as the egg whites hit the right consistency. She stared down into the fluffy white mixture for a few seconds before replying. "Okay, fine. I'm interested."

Charlie jumped onto the balls of her feet happily. "Thought so. Okay, let me set the scene."

Bria groaned and pulled the mixing bowl from the machine.

Charlie was undeterred. "So, it's a dark night in Young Ms. Kemp's speakeasy—"

"*Young* Ms. Kemp?" Bria asked, incredulous.

"Right, sorry. It's 1922."

"Oh, come the fuck on." She glared at Charlie before grabbing a spatula and carefully folding the egg whites into her batter.

"What?" Charlie cried. "I'm giving you context."

Bria should've known Charlie would make this an entire production when all she wanted to know was why Sully hadn't texted her back! But she couldn't tell Charlie why she was interested unless she wanted half the town to know immediately after opening, so she pressed her lips shut and waited for the other woman to get to the damn point.

"The coppers heard someone in town was running rum," Charlie said dramatically, sounding like Robert Stack on helium.

Charlie didn't so much help Bria prep for the day as use the kitchen as her stage to dramatically recreate nearly a hundred years of Sea Port gossip. Or history. Whatever. Sea Port High School didn't have a great theater program, but she just knew Charlie must have put that department through the ringer. And now Charlie was her problem.

She slid the last tray of donuts into the display case with nearly ten minutes to spare before Confections opened. Their early morning regulars had congregated outside, but Mary still hadn't shown up. According to Charlie, Bria shouldn't expect to see her before noon.

"Are you sure about all this?" Bria asked, walking around to the door. The crowd shifted in preparation, clearly hoping they'd open early, but Bria shook her head — Confections never opened early. Instead, Bria inspected the look of the display case from the customer point of view. Mary never unlocked the door without making sure their cases looked mouthwatering. That wasn't a metric Bria knew exactly how to replicate, but she'd eat everything in the cases, so that was a start.

And apparently, Charlie would as well. She slid one case open and stuck a gloved finger into the bottom row, snatching a jelly donut from the tray and taking a big bite.

"You know you're paying for that, right? That one *and* the other ones," Bria clarified.

Charlie gave her a thumbs up. "Worth it," she said with a mouth full of barely chewed pastry.

"Mary doesn't seem like the kind of person to be drunk and wandering around The Grove at midnight," Bria replied, getting back to Charlie's needlessly long story.

"It might not have been midnight, but it was late. And according to my source, she was *very* drunk."

"And who's your source?"

"Confidential," Charlie muttered just before she took another bite of her purloined donut.

"How do you even know about Old Ms. Kemp's speakeasy? I didn't know until last night."

"Also confidential."

"Why was the Mayor there?"

Charlie shrugged.

"What did your source have to say about her?"

Charlie licked a smear of jelly from the corner of her mouth. "Not much. Just that she was there and didn't seem to be in a good mood. She was whispering to your girlfriend, though. It looked serious."

"She's not my girlfriend," Bria said. She let the 'unfortunately' hang in the silence.

"Sure. Anyway, all I know is Mayor Waltham didn't look like herself. According to my source, she didn't have that air about her."

Charlie didn't need to explain; Bria knew exactly what she meant. "Waltham Perfect."

"Exactly. But thankfully, your friend who's a girl..." she said, laughing when Bria rolled her eyes. "Thanks to Sully, Santos didn't arrest her."

"You really think he would've arrested the Mayor?" Bria gasped.

Charlie smirked, but before she could reply, they both heard the back door open. Bria's eyes went wide and she rushed to the swinging door to the kitchen. Someone, probably Ms. Ford, knocked impatiently on the front door. They still had five minutes before the doors unlocked, so Bria ignored her. Charlie rushed to the swinging door, still nibbling on her donut, and pushed it open cautiously. Neither was prepared for what they saw.

In the two years Bria had known Mary, she'd never arrived at Confections with anything less than sunshine hot on her heels. Bria didn't know how Mary did it, but no matter how early she walked into the bakery, she always had a smile on her face. Until today.

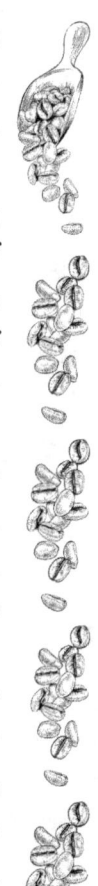

The Mary who walked into Confections this morning four minutes to opening looked like a rainy-day version of herself. She wore dark sunglasses pushed high on her face and held a travel cup of coffee in one hand and a liter of water in the other, both clutched close to her chest like they were the only things keeping her standing and conscious. She wasn't even dressed like herself. Instead of her regular comfortable leggings and oversized t-shirt, she was wearing a pair of baggy sweatpants and a tight hoodie with 'MARINES' stitched on the front. She also looked like she might just keel over any minute.

"Told you," Charlie whispered only loud enough for Bria and Mary to hear. Charlie had never been shy about her nosiness. "Word on the street is the Mayor, the Baker, the Librarian, and the Proprietor of Sea Port's only coffee shop were all out causing mayhem in The Grove last night, and the full force of the Sea Port Police Department had to break it up."

Mary stared at them, swaying slightly where she stood. "I plead the fifth."

Charlie sucked her teeth in annoyance. "The one freaking night something interesting happens in this place and I miss it."

"Lower your voice," Mary whined. "Dear god, why is this place so bright?"

"Remind me to never mess with the Kemp bourbon," Bria whispered.

"Or the gin," Mary added. "Silent killer." And then she perked up for a second. "Do we have any bagels?" She lowered her glasses to the tip of her nose and aimed a piercing, pathetic stare directly at Bria. "Please tell me you made bagels."

There had been odd days at Confections, but this seemed to be the start of a very strange one indeed. "There's a batch of egg bagels in the warmer. I can whip up some cream cheese too if you want it."

"I do," Mary moaned. The sound was somewhere between desperate and sexual and it made Bria and Charlie laugh.

"Shhh," Mary hissed. "Please bring many bagels to my office. If I'm asleep, just leave them on my desk as close to my mouth as possible." She nodded slowly and swayed forward a step before shuffling into her small office closet and closing the door.

"Maybe don't tell the gossip mill that Mary is such a wreck today," Bria whispered.

"Wish I could stop the Natural Order of Nosy, friend, but I guarantee that this has already hit the WAKC phone tree," Charlie replied.

Bria nodded sadly, knowing she was right. Poor Mary. She'd just gotten off of the top of the town gossip list.

Unfortunately, Bria didn't have time to wallow on her boss's behalf. An insistent knock on the shop's front door pulled their attention back to the storefront where Mrs. Lee refused to be put off. She came in once a week to pick up two dozen muffins she passed off as her own at the Church Ladies' breakfast and nothing — not Mary's hangover or Bria and Charlie's nosiness — would make her late for Jesus.

"Coming!" Charlie yelled, popping the last of the donut into her mouth.

Bria grabbed Charlie by the waist. "Go wash your hands," she ground out, stepping around her and rushing to open the door.

Confections was now open for business.

WELCOME TO SEA PORT

SEVENTEEN

Sully

S ully didn't have family drama on today's to-do list.

She was hoping to flirt with Bria over a bagel and a donut, handle her budget for real, and then take Bria out on another date. That was it. If she also found time for a midday nap, she would've been ecstatic. Her day had almost started perfectly.

She woke up right on time, a little dehydrated but clear-headed. She was up, dressed, and ready to go when Bria finally replied to the text message she'd sent right before falling asleep last night. But it was as if the universe never wanted her to be *too* happy because right when she was about to ask Bria out on their second date, Celia Waltham came knocking on her door. And now she was sitting in Willie's kitchen, trying to blend into the wallpaper while the Waltham women argued fiercely.

Sully was staring at the floor, afraid to look at either woman as they yelled across the small kitchen. She tried to close her ears to their family squabble, but every time she let her mind wander, all she could think about was Bria. Terrible timing.

"Why didn't you tell me?"

"You were just a child," Celia replied with a dismissive wave of her hand.

"I've been grown for a while."

"Grown?" Celia scoffed. "You still need me to make sure there's food in your refrigerator. And with this outburst..."

"It's not an outburst," Willie said, struggling not to raise her voice at her mother.

"What else would you call your behavior? You've been refusing to accept my calls for weeks."

Sully had known Celia for years, but she wasn't particularly close to her. She was supportive and could be warm when she wanted, but she was also standoffish. Sully didn't take her behavior personally, though, because she was like that with almost everyone, even Willie at the wrong time. This was the wrong time. Celia's voice was cold and dismissive and made Sully flinch. And if it stung Sully, she couldn't imagine how Willie felt.

She shifted her gaze from the cracked tile at the base of the kitchen island to Willie's face. If she was hurt, she didn't let it show, but Sully knew there was *something* happening underneath the surface when Willie spoke in a shaking voice.

"I'm refusing your calls because I'm not ready to talk to you," Willie said. Her words were careful, clipped.

"Why? It's not like I did anything wrong."

"I didn't say you did. I... I don't understand. Daddy ch-cheated on you and you just...let him?" Willie was one of the smartest people Sully knew and it was rare to see her struggle to understand something. Besides the hurt and the anger, Sully could also see Willie trying to wrap her brain around this new information and it was tearing her apart.

Sully was sitting just behind Celia, so she saw the older woman's back stiffen.

"So his cheating was my responsibility?" Celia spat back. "I thought I raised you better than that."

Willie balled her fists at her sides. "You did, which is why I can't understand why you'd ever stay with a man who cheated on you." Sully mentally clapped for Willie. She couldn't imagine being nearly this coherent if she'd found out her own father cheated on her mom, and she barely liked them.

The quiet was maddening. Sully wanted to crawl out of her skin for ten whole seconds.

"He didn't cheat," Celia said, her voice barely above a whisper.

Willie let out a rough burst of air dripping in disbelief.

The kitchen went quiet again.

"Your father and I... We had a— What do you kids call it these days?" She turned to Sully, snapping her fingers.

Sully's eyes went wide and she shook her head. "I don't know," she said with her hands in the air. "I've been single for like five years."

Celia sucked her teeth and turned back to her daughter. "We had an agreement," she said, snapping her fingers one more time. "He had his dalliances and I had mine."

"Mama!" Willie gasped.

"What? Isn't that exactly what the baker, the police chief, and that good-looking young Knox have going on?"

For the first time since she came downstairs, Willie and

Sully's gazes clashed together. There was entirely too much happening in that sentence for either of them to process.

Willie's attention shifted back to her mother. "If it was so normal, why didn't you ever tell me I had a sister? If everything was so above board, why did I have to find out about this by accident?" It was subtle, but Sully heard the emotion — the slightest hitch — in her voice.

For the first time in all the years she'd known her, Sully saw the ever-calm Celia wilt slightly, and only for a second. She lifted her chin slightly before she spoke.

"Your father was not a perfect man. None of us are perfect people," Celia began, her eyes darting around the room as if she were pulling the words from the atmosphere. "I had absolutely no problem with your father carrying on with Evelyn Stone. She's actually a wonderful woman, God-fearing, kind— so long as they were discreet. A baby out of wedlock was *not* discreet. And it was an election year..." Celia trailed off as if those words explained everything.

Willie reared back as if she'd been slapped. "So you and daddy were going to keep her a secret from me forever?" she asked, her voice rising in frustration and volume.

"In all honesty," Celia said, managing to look annoyed and regal at the same time, "we didn't think that far ahead and then we just ran out of time. Evelyn decided on her own to leave town before she started to show and we didn't stop her. She returned a few years later with a daughter and a story about a long-haul trucker. We all decided to let sleeping dogs lie."

Sully caught the tense grinding of Willie's jaw before she replied. "Then why did you put her name in Aunt Amy's bible?"

Celia sighed dramatically. "I thought no one would notice it for a long while. No one's opened that thing in decades," she said.

Sully had a hard time understanding that logic, but none of this was her business. She hated that she even had to hear it before Willie was ready to share, so she decided to leave. Celia wanted Sully to let her into Willie's half of the duplex; she had. Willie wanted her to stay while she talked to her mother, and she'd done that as well, but now it was time for her to leave. She had a coffee shop to run, a life to live, and she hated learning about Bria's childhood like this.

Sully slipped from Willie's front door just as the strained conversation between mother and daughter finally erupted into raised, broken voices. She jogged down the steps, running from their cries as fast as she could.

The short walk to the coffee shop seemed longer because Sully's mind was working the entire way. She wanted to text Bria, but how could she? What could she say to her now that she knew so much? How could she smile in her face, flirt with her, kiss her and more, with the burden of all those Waltham secrets cluttering her mind?

Secrets Bria, of all people, deserved to know.

S ully had never been happier to see anyone as she was when she spotted Keith behind the register.

"You're late," he called to her.

"I know," Sully groaned, stomping behind the counter. "My morning got away from me."

"Is that code for something?" he asked.

She moved to the espresso machine, hoping caffeine would erase the last half an hour of her life. The familiar sounds of the coffee shop — grinding beans, the high-pitched wail of the milk frother, the persistent din of Portie chatter undercut by the smooth jazz on Keith's playlist for the day — soothed Sully's nerves, but only for a second.

She glanced at Keith over her shoulder. Bria's best friend was refilling the napkin dispensers while humming to the music. Sully had understood that Sea Port was a small town but this was the moment it hit her just how small. She'd just ran away from Willie's family drama about Bria only to find herself face-to-face with Bria's closest friend. If she decided to take a walk around the block to clear her head, she'd pass Bria's job. There was nowhere to run away from her presence, not that she wanted to.

The oddest part of it all was that Bria was a couple blocks away, completely unaware that her existence was ripping Willie's life apart.

There was no way for her to answer Keith's question honestly.

"It's code for I overslept," she mumbled once the espresso machine stopped screaming at her.

"So it's true, huh?" Keith laughed, moving to the prep sink to wash his hands.

She set her espresso cup to the side and started to clean the machine, but his words gave her pause. "What's true?"

He grabbed two paper towels from the dispenser above

the sink. "I heard you and the Mayor got picked up on a drunk and disorderly last night."

"What?" Sully shrieked.

"Heard they had to drag Santos out of bed to pick you up from the farms out past The Grove."

"I didn't get arrested last night. Or ever. I've never been arrested. I've never been arrested in Sea Port," she said, correcting herself in the end.

"Sure. Okay," Keith replied, amused but unconvinced.

"Who told you that?"

"Charlie," he said, giving up his source quickly without an ounce of hesitation.

"Who'd she hear it from?" Sully asked.

Keith shrugged. "No one knows Charlie's sources, but half the town will know by this afternoon."

"What about Mary? And Lorraine?" Sully asked incredulously. "They were there too."

"Yeah, I heard," Keith said nonchalantly. "But *you* were with Mayor Waltham. I'd be surprised if this doesn't come up at the next City Council meeting."

"You're kidding me," Sully said.

"Welcome to small-town living," he laughed, shaking his head.

"Here she is."

Sully turned at the greeting and found Mr. Genova waving at her. She forced a smile on her face, still confused that people thought she got arrested but came to work right after. She'd never.

"Um, hi. Hey. I mean good morning, Mr. Genova. How are you?" She needed coffee and ten minutes of complete silence.

"Good morning to you too. Call me Sal," he replied happily.

"Can't do that, Mr. Genova. We're in the South."

"Oh, I like her."

Sully's gaze shifted to the woman next to him and immediately knew who she was. Bria looked like her mother had copy-and-pasted herself.

Apparently, there was nowhere Sully could go in Sea Port to escape Bria.

Sully's throat felt like it would close. "Ma'am. Uh...good morning?" she stammered out.

"Good morning. Do you know who I am, young lady?" She lifted her chin as she spoke and looked down the bridge of her nose. It was a subtle shift, but that little tilt of her head made the stark contrast between her and her daughter very clear.

"Yes, ma'am, I do," Sully replied, rushing around the counter quickly. She wiped her hand on the back of her pants leg and offered it to Bria's mother. "It's a pleasure to meet you finally."

They stared at one another for a few seconds, Sully's hand hanging between them. Sully bit her lips shut while she waited. Finally, Bria's mother extended her hand and gripped Sully's firmly, but not too tight. Just enough to let Sully know that Bria was loved; Bria was not alone.

"My name is Evelyn Stone, but most everybody calls me Ms. Evie. You may as well."

"Yes, ma'am. I mean, Ms. Evie."

"I told you she was a good one," Mr. Genova said, tapping the side of his nose.

"Oh, hush you," Ms. Evie said with a playful swat at his

shoulder. "Are you going to buy me this tea you've been promising me or not?"

"I'll buy you tea and cake and cookies and everything you want, my dear," Mr. Genova sang at her. His face was light and playful, but Sully could see that he was one hundred percent serious, another thing that was none of her business.

"Not you two flirting in public like this," Keith sighed in disgust.

"Excuse me?" Ms. Evie warned.

"Nothing, ma'am," he said and then rushed away to buss tables.

"What kind of tea would you like? It's on the house."

"I think she's trying to butter us up," Ms. Evie whispered to Mr. Genova.

"Well, in that case, we'll take a piece of cake to share," he said with a playful wink.

"Sure thing. Just let me know what you want and I'll bring it out to you," she said before rushing back behind the counter.

Sully took a few deep breaths and her mind went immediately to Bria — the night they'd spent together, Willie's sad eyes about her, Willie yelling at Celia about her, Keith, and now even Ms. Evie. Her throat felt full of all the things she wanted to say to Bria, and most of the list wasn't even hers to share.

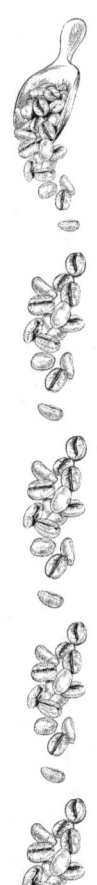

WELCOME TO SEA PORT

EIGHTEEN

Bria

Sully hadn't texted her all morning, and now she was pissed. She was also annoyed because Mary and Charlie were eating all the damn donut holes before they could cool. But this was Mary's bakery, so being mad at her felt strange, and being mad at Charlie was like being mad at the wind — she did not care. And both women were on a sugar high so serious, they'd probably forgotten Bria even existed hours ago. There was a solid period during her lunch break when Bria tried to be mad at Sully, but she still wanted to kiss her, so she took her frustration out on some bread dough instead.

By early afternoon, Mary was back on her feet. A little wobbly, but strong enough to wash dishes and help Bria clean the kitchen.

"I got this," Mary said when Bria started loading the dishwasher.

"Oh, okay. I'll do the bathroom then," Bria replied.

Mary shook her head and then closed her eyes. She

swayed lightly and breathed through whatever wave of sickness she felt. She opened her eyes and smiled weakly. "I'll have Charlie do it."

That brightened Bria's mood. "Oh, good."

"And you can go home. You've done enough today," Mary said carefully. "I'll be happy to leave the bakery in your hands while I'm gone for the holidays."

Bria's face lit up. "So you're going?"

"Nothing's set in stone yet, but probably, yeah."

"Santos and Knox are gonna be so happy," Bria squealed.

"Yeah, I know. Now go. You deserve a break."

"Thanks," Bria said, trying not to freak out just yet. She washed up and grabbed her bag before skipping out the front door, leaving all the morning's frustrations with her because she walked straight into Sully.

Fucking finally!

SULLY

Sully hated secrets, and she hated lying even more. Willie knew this about her, so she had to have known that Sully would fold. Or at least that's what Sully told herself as she walked to Confections.

When she left the coffee shop, she'd planned to go to Willie's office, but she ended up at Confections instead. She stood across the street and stared at the storefront for at least a full minute before she finally got the nerve to cross at a light jog. The door opened as Sully reached for it and Bria practically skipped into her arms.

Somehow, she hadn't seen Bria since they fell asleep together, but it didn't feel like that. As soon as Sully saw her again, it was like they'd spent no time apart. She'd somehow felt every hour of their separation and it flew by in a breath. For a brief moment, all the anxiety of the last day evaporated and a tension eased from Sully's shoulders in the light of Bria's bright smile.

Bria pulled the door closed behind her and stepped onto the curb. "Hello."

"Hey. Hi," Sully stammered.

"Oh, look, two words you could've texted me..." She lifted her arm to check the time on her bare wrist. "Hours ago," she finished.

"You're right," Sully smiled.

"Oooh, I love hearing that."

"Would you believe me if I said I meant to text you back?" Sully took a quick step closer.

"I would, actually," she said. "With an explanation."

Sully nodded but the bakery door opened before she could speak.

"Bria, don't leave," Charlie gasped, leaning through the door.

"Why?" Bria sucked her teeth in frustration.

"She wants me to clean the bathroom," Charlie whined.

"Well, that is part of your job."

"But my nails are already a wreck." She lifted a hand to show them.

Sully thought Charlie's hands looked fine.

"There are gloves under the sink," Bria said, stepping around Sully and pulling her down the street, their fingers sliding together.

"Ugh, fine. Fine! But when I start dating somebody, remember this moment!"

"I will!" Bria yelled back.

"You sure you don't want to stay?" Sully laughed.

"Tempting, but I'm gonna pass."

She pulled Bria into her side and slid her arm around Bria's waist. She ducked her head but Sully saw the curve of her smile. "Do you have anywhere to be right now?" she whispered.

"You'd know the answer to that if you'd texted me back this morning," Bria teased.

"I already said you were right."

"Can't hurt to hear it again," Bria whispered.

"If it'll make you feel better."

"It would," Bria said quickly, turning to smile at her.

"Willie needed my help this morning and then I had to rush to the coffee shop," Sully said, skirting along the edges of telling the full truth.

"Does the Mayor normally occupy so much of your time?" Bria asked.

"No," Sully replied definitively. "These are—" She stopped, searching for the best words to describe the weirdest day of her life. "These are very strange circumstances. If I'd known this was coming, I would've gotten the nerve to ask you out months ago."

"God, I wish we'd done that earlier."

Sully tilted her head to whisper in Bria's ear. "You're right."

"It's easier every time you say it," Bria laughed.

Sully brushed her lips against Bria's cheek. "I can keep telling you you're right," she said. Bria nodded quickly. "Or I can make it up to you."

"Oooh," Bria sighed. "I'm listening."

"The goal is to stop speaking, actually."

"Sounds very good to me," Bria laughed. "Your place is closer."

Sully let Bria pull her for a few steps before she stopped, thinking about the scene she'd left in Willie's half of the duplex this morning. "Um, actually, can we go to your place?"

Bria turned around, confusion etched onto her face. "You remember I live with my mom, right?"

"I remember. Oh, she was at the coffee shop earlier."

"She was?"

"Yeah. She was with Mr. Genova. I think they came to check me out. Officially."

Bria rolled her eyes. "They definitely did that," she sighed, but then her face lit up. "But if they're together, she's gonna go to Sal's and help with pre-dinner prep, so we have time."

She threw her arm around Sully's waist and pulled her forward. "Come on. Let's break my bed in."

"Bria, oh my god," Sully gasped, laughing so hard she snorted.

BRIA

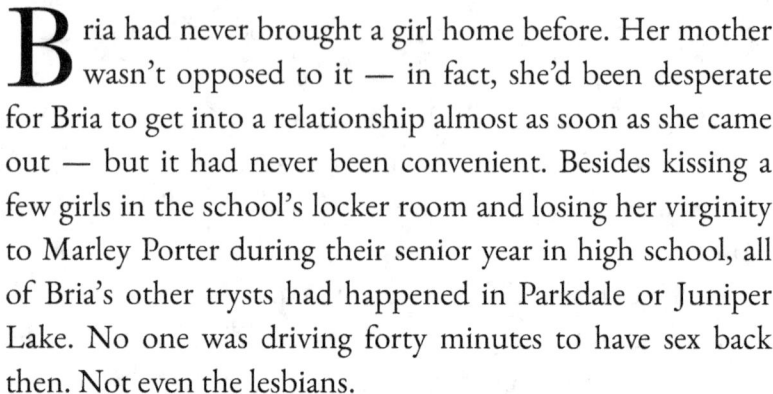

Bria had never brought a girl home before. Her mother wasn't opposed to it — in fact, she'd been desperate for Bria to get into a relationship almost as soon as she came out — but it had never been convenient. Besides kissing a few girls in the school's locker room and losing her virginity to Marley Porter during their senior year in high school, all of Bria's other trysts had happened in Parkdale or Juniper Lake. No one was driving forty minutes to have sex back then. Not even the lesbians.

But Sully was local!

She let Sully into the small cottage she shared with her mom, nervously excited about the gravity of this moment.

"We take our shoes off at the door," Bria whispered, even though no one was home.

Sully nodded and toed off her sneakers before nudging them neatly out of the way. Bria was much less neat, taking her shoes off where she stood and dropping her keys into a bowl atop a credenza just inside the living room. She turned to invite Sully further into the house but watched her use her foot to move Bria's shoes out of the way of the door.

"Oh, I bet my mama *loved* you," she whispered, her heart pounding against her chest.

Sully's cheeks flushed. "I gave her a piece of cake on the house." She was standing just inside the living room, her hands shoved into her pants pockets and a small, sexy smile on her face that was playing havoc on Bria's hormones.

"Yeah, she loved you," Bria breathed, trying not to betray how happy that made her.

Bria loved watching Sully move. If it wouldn't have been

so obvious, Bria would've spent her lunch breaks in the coffee shop just watching Sully work — shoving her hands in her pants pockets while she chatted with the members of WAKC, pushing her sleeves up to her elbows, smoothing a hand over the crown of her head. She used to close her eyes and just imagine Sully leaning against the wall, talking to Knox or sipping an espresso and licking it from her lips. That's when she knew she had it bad.

"Follow me," she whispered and turned away as her stomach clenched in lust. The living room led straight into the dining room and kitchen with two bedrooms on one side and her mother's larger bedroom on the other, giving both women privacy in the small house. Besides the fact that Bria didn't want to move out of her mother's home, she didn't need to — not yet, at least.

She pushed open her bedroom door and dropped her bag in the desk chair she mostly used for storage. Bria's room wasn't dirty — Evelyn Stone would've never allowed that — she just wasn't the tidiest person in the world. Normally she didn't care, but today she wished she'd at least straightened up a little. She kicked some clothes under the bed, threw her comforter over her rumpled sheets, and slammed her laptop closed.

"Just gimme a sec," Bria breathed, glancing at Sully over her shoulder.

Sully leaned against the doorjamb and dipped her head to hide her smile.

"Don't laugh."

"I'm not laughing," Sully said, even though her shoulders were jumping with suppressed giggles.

Bria threw last night's pajamas into her hamper while

Sully wiped the tears from her cheeks. "If I'd known you were coming over, I'd have done a little tidying. I promise."

"I believe you," she managed to say before another fit of giggles took her down.

Bria took advantage of Sully's closed eyes to quickly straighten her bedside table. Her room still looked a mess, but at least she tried.

"You're adorable," Sully laughed.

"Yeah? Just adorable?" Bria asked.

Sully's hand moved down her chin and loosely circled her throat. She shook her head as her gaze moved over Bria's body.

Bria moved her hands just under the hem of her t-shirt and Sully licked her lips. "Come here," Bria whispered.

Sully closed the door behind her and stepped toward Bria with slow, deliberate steps. She lifted her hand to the hem of Bria's shirt and smoothed two fingers along the cotton before touching her wrist. "So you missed me today?" Sully asked as she covered the back of Bria's hand with her palm.

"Maybe." Bria licked her dry lips.

Sully's skin was warm, the pads of her fingers were callused, and Bria's pulse was racing as she remembered how good and strong her fingers had felt two nights ago. She wanted to make new memories.

Sully used both hands to pull Bria's shirt over her head, but she did it slowly, dragging her knuckles along Bria's skin — up her ribs, around the sides of her breasts.

"Did you miss me?" Bria asked as Sully's hands caressed her waist and she leaned forward.

"Yes," Sully replied against Bria's lips.

That one word became a gentle kiss and Bria sighed into Sully's mouth. She offered the tip of her tongue and Sully accepted that and more. Their first night was frantic, desperate — so many months of yearning finally finding a release — but this felt different.

They knew each other in a way they hadn't before and it showed in each kiss, every touch, every item of clothing they stripped from one another. They touched each other like they'd been thinking about that night on a loop because they had.

Bria caressed the back of her neck until Sully practically purred against her tongue. Sully's fingers danced up Bria's spine, tickling her until she brushed her breasts against Sully's chest.

If this was Bria's reward for all her hard work this morning, it was worth it.

SULLY

Sully hadn't gotten to see all of Bria in her dark bedroom. She caught glimpses of her up close — the dimple in her left cheek, the small mole on her inner thigh, the small keloid scar on her hip — but not the full picture. But in Bria's bright bedroom, Sully saw everything.

She walked Bria to the bedroom door, turned her around, and lifted Bria's hands to the wood. She kissed her right shoulder while her hands skimmed along her hips before stepping back to admire the view. Sully caressed Bria's ass, while her right foot pushed the other woman's feet apart.

A shiver moved through Bria's body and a low moan fell from her lips as Sully's fingers brushed her pussy from behind.

"Oooh," Bria cooed softly as she lifted onto the balls of her feet.

"You nervous?" Sully lifted her hand to caress Bria's shoulder and stepped into the space between her spread legs.

"Impatient." Bria arched her back and turned her head to brush her mouth along Sully's jaw.

"I know the feeling," Sully laughed as her hands moved forward to Bria's chest. She cupped her breasts from the side and gently massaged them while Bria sighed against the door for a second. But only a second before Sully pulled Bria back into her chest.

Bria reached back and grabbed onto Sully's ass for stability. They laughed together and then Bria moaned when Sully's fingers quickly brushed her distended nipples. For the next few minutes, Sully alternated between massaging Bria's breasts and toying with her nipples, playing with her as if they had all day. As if there weren't secrets troubling the waters just outside Bria's bedroom door.

"Just relax," Sully whispered.

"I'm relaxed," Bria said. "But I'd be more relaxed if you stopped teasing me."

Sully pressed her mouth against Bria's, smiling against her lips while she rolled Bria's nipples between her fingers. Her moans tasted like heaven.

"Good?" Sully whispered.

Bria squirmed in her arms and sucked Sully's tongue into her mouth.

Sully reluctantly let go of Bria's right breast and tickled a path over her stomach. She teased her fingers across Bria's mound, brushed her hooded clit, and then spread her fingers along the cleft of her pussy, holding her sex possessively in the palm of her hand. Her other hand was on the move, tickling Bria's side, caressing her hips and then pushing between her legs from the back. Sully used both hands to get Bria off, fingers strumming her clit while the other hand fucked her hole. She deserved no less.

Everything that wasn't Bria ceased to exist for the next hour and it was beautiful.

Only Sully knew that this kind of peace couldn't last.

WELCOME TO SEA PORT

NINETEEN

Willie

Willie had been staring at her computer for so long she couldn't even remember what she was supposed to be typing.

She scrubbed her face and blinked at the screen before remembering that she was supposed to be working through another batch of Transplant applications, normally her favorite part of any day. When Willie first proposed the project to the City Council, almost everyone believed it would fail, even some of the people who eventually voted to approve it later. But in just a few short years, the Sea Port Relocation Initiative wasn't just working, it was working a little *too* well. Three years ago, she'd log into the portal to review applications once or twice every other week — sometimes less — but these days she got notifications of new applications multiple times a day. Willie knew the time was quickly approaching when she'd need to hire some help, but delegating was one of Willie's weak points if she had any.

She normally enjoyed skimming through the applications to remind herself of just how much progress Sea Port had made in her short tenure as Mayor, but she couldn't focus today. She wanted to be excited about the nurse applying to run the clinic they'd just secured funding to renovate or the has-been chef who wanted to bring fine dining to Sea Port, but the minute she started reading their résumés, her brain would immediately drift to Bria. Her sister.

Willie had a sister.

Her father was a cheater.

All roads led back to the shattered image of her father, crushing a small part of her soul — the part that would always be a daddy's girl; his twin. She knew her father wasn't perfect, but the man who raised her wasn't a cheater — at least he wasn't supposed to be. But he was, and being reminded of his failures — and her mother's too, apparently — was too much for her to handle today.

Willie closed the application portal and then turned her computer off entirely. She needed some fresh air.

She pulled open her office door to find Santos and Knox standing in the foyer. There was a desk for a secretary Willie's office couldn't afford right now and Knox was sitting on it, one leg bent and the other foot planted firmly on the old dark blue carpet that had been there since Willie was a child.

"Can I help you?" Willie asked, trying not to sound annoyed at their presence. Her current predicament wasn't their fault. Knox gave her a big, wide smile and she rolled her eyes. "I'm immune. Knock it off."

Knox's smile faltered and Santos dipped his head to hide

his soft laughter. He rolled his eyes at Santos and stood from the desk. "We wanted to talk about public safety."

"What about it?"

Santos cleared his throat. "There's not enough streetlights."

Willie's face bunched together. "We barely have streets, so..."

Both men nodded.

"Still," Knox said, "if we're gonna have people, uh...out at night, especially in the more rural areas, we'd both feel better if there were at least a few lampposts." He was dancing around last night and neither man could look her in the eyes, but she had more serious matters on her mind than public intoxication.

"That makes sense," she said. "Give me a proposal and budget by the end of next week and I'll attach it to the city development proposal for our angel investor. Now, if you'll excuse me," she said, stepping forward and forcing Knox to jump out of her way.

Willie started walking without a destination in mind and ended up at Sully's café, looking for anything to take her mind off the fight with her mother. Keith was behind the register but there was no Sully in sight. Willie scanned the room, looking for her best friend, but saw Ms. Evie instead.

In a town as small as Sea Port and with so few kids, Willie remembered Bria, but she had far clearer images of Bria's mother — not enough to be close to the woman, but enough to have all she knew wiped away when she found out about Ms. Evie's affair with her father.

Her feet moved without her mind or body's knowledge or consent.

"Hey there, Mayor Willie," Mr. Genova said cheerily. Under normal circumstances, Mr. Genova was one of Willie's favorite Porties, but all her attention and energy were on Ms. Evie today.

"Does Bria even know she's my sister?" Willie whispered in a broken, angry hiss.

BRIA

Her skin was still cooling down from the shower, but watching Sully pull one of her t-shirts over her head had her heating up again. It was a cute one from Bria's senior spirit week and she felt something primal and possessive seeing Sully wearing it.

"What?" Sully asked as she slipped her belt through the loops of her pants.

"What?" Bria asked, biting back a smile.

"Why are you looking at me like that?"

Bria leaned back, her palms sinking into the mattress. "You want a reminder?" she teased.

Sully's hands stilled and a shy smile lifted her mouth. She was thinking about it — thinking about it so hard, her eyes dipped into small slits and she licked her lips. Bria was thinking about it as well, but seeing Sully's interest had her ready to get undressed again.

But then they both heard the front door slam shut and

their eyes shifted to Bria's closed bedroom door. Bria's eyes went wide and she froze in shock. Sully, however, started moving at double speed, rushing to redress. Bria heard her mother's heavy footsteps in the hallway and she finally jumped up from her bed and rushed to the door. She pulled it open before her mother had a chance to knock — no one knew better than Bria that the best way to face her mother was head-on. She opened the door far enough that her mother could see Sully behind her. Her mom's face shifted in surprise, but only for a second before her expression bunched together in frustration.

"What's up, mama?"

"Hi, Ms. Evie," Sully said. Her voice shook a little.

"I need to talk to you," her mother said.

"Okay. Can it wait 'cause...?"

"No." Her eyes shifted to the carpet for a few seconds before she lifted her head. Bria didn't like the look in her mother's eyes. "This has waited long enough. Meet me in the living room," she said, turning around and walking back toward the front of the house without another word.

"Mama?" Bria watched her mother walk down the hall with stooped shoulders and fear shot through her veins. "Am I in trouble?" she asked, even though she was an adult.

Sully's hand settled on her shoulder and squeezed.

"I didn't do anything, I swear," Bria laughed, still confused.

"I'm sure you didn't," Sully said, smiling but not laughing.

"Come on, I'll walk you out," Bria whispered, feeling like the ground was shifting right under her feet.

She led Sully down the hallway. It was a short walk and

Bria used every inch of carpet to wrack her brain about what could have her mother in a mood, but she was coming up empty. She was even more confused when she turned into the living room only to find Mayor Waltham standing just inside their front door, heels off and a pensive look on her face.

"What are you doing here?" Sully asked before Bria could think to speak.

Mayor Waltham's face was stone. "What are *you* doing here?"

Bria didn't like her tone. "I invited her. Not that it's any of your business."

Mayor Waltham's gaze moved to Bria and the frustration on her face shifted to an expression that was pensive and unsure.

"I invited Mayor Waltham," Evelyn replied tersely.

Bria shrugged. "Okay."

"We need to talk."

"Okay. Let me just walk Sully out and you can talk to her and then—"

Her mother shook her head. "No, I mean the three of us need to speak. You, me, and the Mayor."

"Willie," Mayor Waltham corrected.

Bria didn't have any reason to speak to Mayor Waltham. Most of their interactions were in passing, usually at City Council meetings whenever Sal forced her to go with him. She usually sounded professional, her Southern accent hardly more than a slight inflection, but she sounded different today — more like a regular Portie, or something close to it.

"I should go," Sully whispered.

Bria shook her head stubbornly, which she would say was a Stone family weakness if she was forced to name a weakness at all. "You can stay," she replied, but her attention was focused on her mother.

"Sit down, dumpling," her mother said in the voice she used whenever she had to be the bearer of bad news.

Bria shook her head as a sense of dread started building in her gut. "What's going on?"

Sully's hand was back on her shoulder, and the squeeze was a small comfort.

"Bria," her mother started, but then her voice gave out. She twisted her fingers together nervously.

"Mama?"

Her mother sucked in a big gulp of air, then released it and started again. "Bria, I want to talk to you about your father."

When she was younger, Bria used to ask a million questions about her dad before she realized it was pointless; before she realized that her mother could lie. Every story her mother had ever told her about the father she never met was fantastical, painting him as a larger-than-life figure for Bria to idolize and miss, but not think too hard about. It had worked for a while — a long while — until one day, the scales fell from Bria's eyes. She couldn't even remember what shook a little sense into her, just that one day, she really believed her father was going on adventures in his big rig and the next, she didn't. She was ten years old. Bria stopped asking questions about a man who clearly didn't want to be a father and decided that she didn't want to be his daughter. Giving up on the fairy tale about a man she never knew was

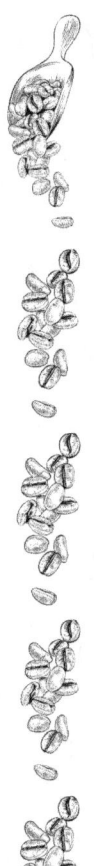

easier than expected. It took a few years before she stopped dreaming about him — or the version of him her mother created in bedtime stories — but it had been years since she even thought about him. Bria had been fatherless her entire life, but many people have survived worse.

"What about him?" Bria asked with a defiant tilt of her chin.

"I've been lying to you for so long. Longer than I ever imagined I would."

"I know," Bria shrugged. "It's fine."

"It's not," her mother replied, shaking her head.

By and large, Evelyn Stone was frustratingly honest, especially with Bria. When Bria asked what Santa would get her for Christmas, Evelyn took her to the mall two towns over and told her she was Santa and they had a budget, so whatever Bria wanted was going on layaway. When Bria came out and worried people at their church might shun her, Evelyn stood up in church the next Sunday to give a testimony — a testimony where she threatened to beat anyone who said a cross word to her daughter through the floorboards. Everyone knew she meant it. Evelyn Stone didn't lie and that was a bedrock concept in Bria's life. And when she did lie, Bria accepted that it must've been for a good reason.

"I stopped believing he was the world's busiest long-haul truck driver years ago," Bria said gently. "It's fine. I know you lied to protect me."

"It's not fine," she said again. "And I didn't lie to protect you. I lied to protect myself because your father wasn't a long-haul trucker, he was a married man."

"What?" The word burst past her lips much louder than Bria wanted.

Evelyn nodded understandingly as she launched into a simple, clear explanation, no excuses. "I was in my early twenties and bored and thought I was so grown. We had an affair for a year and got careless. When I found out I was pregnant, I realized how reckless I'd been. How reckless we'd both been. But at the same time, I was so happy. You were nothing but a cluster of cells and I already knew you were going to be the love of my life."

"Mama, stop," Bria said, feeling and sounding desperate.

Sully squeezed her shoulder, but Bria shook off her touch. She didn't want Sully to touch her, let alone see her, right now.

"Everyone knew what we'd done. And I was...fine with them judging me for what I'd done. I deserved that."

"Mama, stop," Bria said again, shaking her head, wanting desperately for this to be another lie and fearing it wasn't. Knowing it wasn't.

"I didn't care if people judged me for what I'd done because I did it, it was my mistake, but I didn't want them judging you. I wanted to give you whatever cover I could, so I broke it off with your father and left town for a little while. That's why there weren't ever any pictures of me pregnant with you at your grandparents' house. I thought if I left and came back, it would be better than walking around here young, unmarried, and pregnant. We had a life outside of Sea Port for a little while." Her mother laughed dryly, sadly. "That was all I'd ever wanted, and I got it in the most unconventional way."

"Mama?" Bria couldn't think of anything else to say.

Evelyn kept going gently, slowly, but clearly. "For all that time I spent wanting to get the hell out of here, I was lonely. So when you were three, I came back and we started our life over. Everyone still knew who your father was, or guessed who he was, at least, but you're the spitting image of me and your grandmother. You had our last name. You were my baby, no one else's, and everyone just let us pretend because they loved you enough."

Bria's eyes were full of tears by this point. "Who's my father, mama?"

"My father," Mayor Waltham cut in.

Bria had honestly forgotten the other woman was there. She turned toward her as a small river of tears fell over her cheeks. "What?"

She swallowed before she spoke, her eyes darting in Sully's direction. "My father was...your father. We're sisters."

Bria shook her head, refusing to believe that of all things, but then Mayor Waltham's gaze shifted to Sully again, so Bria turned around as well. It took her a few seconds to recognize what she was seeing on Sully's face — a mix of emotions even as guilt overrode everything else.

"You..." She bunched her eyebrows together, trying to focus her vision through tears she couldn't wipe away fast enough. "Did you know?"

Sully's face was bright red, and for the first time in months, she wouldn't look Bria in the eye or speak as she nodded tightly.

Bria was overcome with a wave of anger and betrayal as her gaze moved from one woman to another. But it was her mother's betrayal that stung the worst. Her mother had always been her rock, but when she looked at her, it was like she didn't recognize her anymore. She walked past Evelyn and Willie, keeping her gaze on the front door. She didn't stop to put on shoes; she simply ran barefoot from her mother's house, feeling lost in Sea Port for the first time in her life.

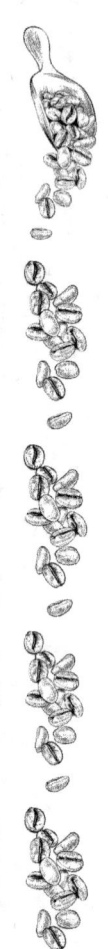

WELCOME TO SEA PORT

TWENTY

Willie

S ully was trying to shove her feet into her shoes while
Willie stood by, stunned and unsure what to do with
herself — let alone anyone else — as she had been for
weeks.

Reading Bria's name in the Waltham family Bible had
shifted the ground she stood on; destabilizing the path her
father had paved for her. Accepting that Bria was her sister
required accepting that her father wasn't the man she
thought she knew, and it had been eating Willie alive. But it
also meant accepting Bria, which was easier than expected.
Willie never minded being an only child, but finding out she
had a sibling — a sister, no less — felt right in a way she
might never have guessed otherwise.

She had wanted to tell Bria, but she never wanted it to
look like this.

"What are you doing?" Ms. Evie asked Sully, looking and
sounding bewildered.

"Going after her," Sully said, shoving her foot into her shoe. Her voice was hard and bordering on disrespectful.

Willie bristled even under the circumstances, but Bria's mother took it in stride.

"That's sweet, but don't do that," she said, smiling sadly.

"Excuse me?" Sully asked, standing straight, that one shoe still hanging onto her toes by a thread.

"Watch your tone," Ms. Evie warned. "I like you, but you're new. When my girl runs away, she's only heading one of two places, Keith's or Sal's."

"Great. Thanks. I'll look for her there since you're not going to."

Willie stepped into one of her pumps before Ms. Evie's face fell into a hard mask.

Ms. Evie stepped forward, close enough that Sully — and by extension, Willie — could see she meant business. "Like I said, you're new. I know my daughter. Let her cool off."

"She doesn't—" Sully started, but Bria's mother wasn't interested in the rest of that sentence.

"You can let her go somewhere where she feels safe to calm down or you can run after her like a superhero and get the brunt of her anger. Pick your poison, but do so from my porch."

It was an elegant way to get kicked out of a house, but Willie was already on the front porch when Ms. Evie picked up Sully's shoe, shoved it against her chest, and then closed the door on both of them. So technically, Sully was the one who got kicked out, not Willie.

Sully looked around the porch in confusion. "What just happened?"

"Your girlfriend's mother kicked you out of her house," Willie sighed. "I didn't think you had it in you."

"But why's she mad at me?"

"Misplaced anger. You want to go find Bria for some more or have you had enough?"

Sully put her hands on her hips, one shoe dangling from her fingers by her still-tied laces. "I just want to know she's okay."

"I get it, but her mom's right. You don't know her well enough to know if this is how she copes. Neither do I."

"So what? You just want to leave her to the wolves?"

Willie laughed. It was dry but full of whatever mirth she could muster in a moment like this. "There aren't any wolves in Sea Port. Not anymore anyway. Sometimes people need space. Let her chill and take it all in. You can run after her like a lovesick puppy tomorrow. Besides, if she's anything like me, she might need a drink or three to cope."

"I'm sorry," Sully whispered. "I know this is a lot for you to handle as well."

Willie nodded and blinked away her tears. "Life is a lot for me to handle right now."

"Fine," Sully said, kicking off her shoe to put it on properly. "I'll leave her alone tonight and stay with you, unless you need to go talk to your mom."

Willie sucked her teeth in annoyance. "I think she and I have said enough to each other for today. Wanna get a drink?"

"Or three?" Sully asked.

"That's the spirit. Hurry up and put your shoes on. Old Ms. Kemp requires shoes and pants for service."

Sully scoffed. "What kind of backyard bar is she running?"

"A reputable one," Willie laughed softly. Sadly.

BRIA

For as long as Bria could remember, Sal's spare bedroom had always been *hers*. She and her mom spent so much time at Sal's restaurant and apartment that Bria thought most homes smelled like tomatoes and garlic. By the time she was a teenager, she'd often drop by Sal's house when she and her mom were fighting to listen to music in peace. Sal was always happy when Bria visited and he never judged her for whatever delinquent thing she'd done. Sal and his apartment were Bria's safe space, but it had been years since she'd needed to use it.

She made her way through Sea Port on muscle memory alone. She walked into the restaurant, only realizing her feet were bare when she stepped on the cool tile in the foyer. Sal was standing at the host station, straightening the stack of menus.

"Sal," she whined softly; the same voice she used when she fell off her bike and wanted him to check her scraped knee.

As always, he didn't miss a beat. He walked around the stand and opened his arms wide. She rushed into his hold without a moment of hesitation and let him hold her, waiting for tears that never came. She felt numb and lost but safe in Sal's arms. He didn't speak or force her to respond, he just waited until Bria could stand on her own two feet and fished his key ring from his pocket.

"Go upstairs," Sal whispered. "I'll check on you later." She nodded and hugged him again, holding tight to the only thing in her life that seemed the same as yesterday.

When she let herself into his apartment, the familiar scent of Pine-Sol and tomatoes engulfed her like a comfortable hug. She walked to her bedroom and finally cried herself to sleep.

WELCOME TO SEA PORT

TWENTY-ONE

Bria

Bria woke up the next morning feeling like shit.

Her head was pounding, her eyes were puffy, and her stomach was grumbling because in all of yesterday's drama, she couldn't even remember eating. She was so damn hungry, her growling stomach woke her out of a dead sleep. The room was tinged a soft blue-gray as sunlight filtered through the thin curtains. She'd always liked the early morning light in this room, even this morning when she could barely see it. Bria rubbed the heels of her hands against her eyes and sat up in bed.

She hadn't heard Sal come home last night, but the signs of his return were obvious — the box fan turned on low and aimed at the bed, just like Bria liked, and a set of towels on the small rocking chair Sal made for her when she was in the sixth grade. She threw the cover from her body and set her feet on the floor.

The awkward weight of her cell phone in her pocket

confused her until she remembered the mess of yesterday. When she pulled the phone free, it was dead as a brick. Bria let out a relieved sigh; she didn't want to talk to anyone right now, especially not her mother. She tossed the phone on the bedside table, grabbed the towels from the chair, and tiptoed across the hall to the bathroom.

Her feet were tender, but Bria felt almost normal once she'd showered. When she looked at her reflection in the foggy bathroom mirror, she saw her mother in her features as always, but today, she leaned forward and searched for any sign of Willie Waltham. Her sister. Just thinking the word made Bria want to run back to the shower and dunk her head under the showerhead this time. If she could've washed away all she'd learned about her family in the last day — against her will, no less — she would have, but that wasn't how life worked.

She kicked the bedroom door closed behind her and walked to the dresser. Bria didn't sleep at Sal's often, but the dresser in her room was stocked with clothes just in case. Just in case she worked late at the restaurant when she was helping out. Just in case someone spilled red wine on her while she was working. Just in case she splashed sauce on herself when she and her mom came over for dinner. Thick socks just in case she walked across town in an emotional haze. She dressed without any urgency, terrified of what the day would throw at her once she left the safety of Sal's apartment.

"There's my girl," Sal called from the kitchen as soon as she pulled the bedroom door open. "Come have some breakfast. You're getting skinny."

Bria padded into the large open plan kitchen-living room area. "I don't eat dinner one night and you think I'm underweight."

He started cracking eggs into a large bowl. "Actually, I've been meaning to tell you this for weeks, but you've been busy. You're not busy now, so I can tell you. You're getting skinny."

She was not. Just yesterday, before everything went to hell, there had been a very brief moment while Sully had Bria's knees pointing toward her own chest when she'd worried what the other woman would think of her soft lower belly pooch, but then Sully had climbed on top of her and pressed their pussies together, using Bria's soft body for leverage. Not only was Bria not getting skinny, she was discovering new uses for all her curves.

Well, she had been, and then her mother had pulled the rug out from under her feet.

"Stop worrying for a few minutes," Sal said, interrupting the speeding train of her thoughts. "Have a seat."

"Yeah, have a seat."

Bria jumped at the sound of another voice in the room. She pressed her left hand to her chest and turned to the living room to find Keith sitting on Sal's couch. "Where the hell did you come from?"

"From home. Obviously." He rolled his eyes as he stood. Keith was wearing his regular uniform of pressed khaki high waters and a printed top. No bowtie today.

"Okay, *what* are you doing here?" she asked.

Her question was punctuated by the sizzling sound of cold vegetables in hot oil. They turned to watch Sal moving around his kitchen, shuffling from the gas stove to his chopping board and back again.

"To see you. *Obviously*," Keith said, accentuating that last word with another roll of his eyes and swiveling neck.

"Did you— Did you know?"

He frowned. "Know what? I heard you and your mom had a fight and he was making omelets. So I'm here."

Bria flung herself into Keith's arms, pressing her cheek just over his heart. She heard him sigh loudly, but since he didn't wrest himself from her tight hold, Bria thought her best friend knew she needed this hug.

"You might not want to hear this," Keith said, "but it was your mom who told me about the omelets and the fight."

The complicated emotions Bria felt at those words were too much for her to process, so she pushed them aside for now. "Thanks for coming," she whispered.

Keith shrugged. "It's my day off."

Bria only let Keith go when the tears building in her eyes threatened to fall down her face. He would kill her if she got tears on his outfit, so she let him go to wipe them on her sleeves.

"Sit, sit," Sal said. "I'm making crepes and vegetable omelets. I might make some sausage too," he added, eyeing her. "You want some sausage, Bria?"

"I'm not getting skinny, Sal. Chill," she laughed, sliding onto a stool at his kitchen island. Keith moved to the fridge and pulled it open, grabbing a carton of orange juice from inside.

Sal slid a few of the most delicate crepes she had ever

seen onto her plate and they ate in silence until some small part of Bria felt like herself again. Unfortunately, as soon as her stomach stopped trying to eat itself, Bria's brain dredged up all that she'd learned yesterday.

Her eyes settled on Sal's back as he carefully folded the large omelet in the skillet.

Bria couldn't remember a day in her life without Sal. She'd sat on this exact stool dozens of times, maybe even hundreds, watching him cook for her like he was her father, which made sense because Sal was the only person in all of Sea Port Evelyn trusted with Bria without reservation. As long as she was with Sal, Evelyn knew Bria would be safe, fed, and heard.

Although, for all Evelyn knew of Sal, somehow, she didn't know how much Sal loved her. He loved Evelyn so much that Bria couldn't remember a day before she knew that as well.

She set her fork down and Sal turned around, skillet in one hand, spatula in the other, to see if she was done. They locked eyes and Bria spoke first.

"How long have you known?" Her voice gave out before the question was complete, but he heard her. She knew it by the way his back stiffened and his mouth turned into a rare frown, but he didn't answer quickly. Sal flipped the omelet onto its own plate and set it between her and Keith to divvy up as they wished. Then he turned off the stove, poured himself a small glass of juice and drank half in one loud gulp, and then looked at Bria again.

"I didn't find out your mother was having an affair with Skip until she told me she was pregnant. I was angry with her

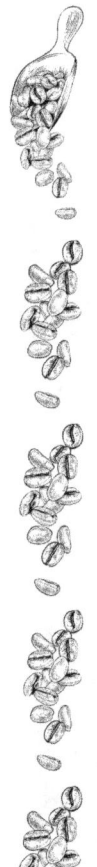

and disappointed. And heartbroken." He stopped to drink the last of his juice. Sal didn't look like himself. Instead of the bright man who'd flipped crepes onto her plate, Sal looked sadder and older than Bria could ever remember him being.

"I wasn't happy with her, but she was my best friend. And the only girl I've ever loved. So when she asked me to help her leave town, I did.

"We packed up everything we thought she'd need. I gave her the five hundred dollars I'd been saving to take her to Atlanta for her next birthday. We'd been planning that trip since we were ten, but it bought your first car seat, so that was fine. Better than fine," he said, smiling at her with glassy eyes.

"Sal," Bria whispered as her own eyes filled with tears. "Why did she lie to me my entire life?"

"You have to ask her that."

"Okay, why did *you* lie to me my whole life?"

He refilled his glass as he spoke. "I think when your mother was with the Mayor, she thought it was romantic. Exciting, at least. If you think Sea Port is boring now, imagine what it was like for us in the Eighties."

Keith gagged lightly and that made Sal smile, however sadly.

"Evelyn always wanted more than Sea Port could give her," he continued.

Bria couldn't help but wonder if he included himself in that statement, but she wasn't bold enough to ask.

"This wasn't the life she wanted, but getting pregnant was good for her. She did a lot of growing up after she had you. It's not my place to judge her for what she did. It's not yours either. I wanted you to see your mother for who she is.

Who she became because of you. I never wanted you to judge her by her worst decision."

"That's bullshit," Bria spat back. "If anyone can judge her, it's me. She spent my entire life lying to me about who my father was."

"Wait, who's your father?" Keith asked.

"Mayor Waltham," Bria said, the words tasting like ash on her tongue.

"Um, isn't she— Oh! Got it. Sorry. Don't mind me," he said, shoveling a forkful of eggs into his mouth.

"She should've told me," Bria aimed at Sal. "Everybody knew but me."

"I didn't know," Keith muttered, but Bria ignored him.

"She just didn't want me to know how stupid and selfish she was—"

"Hey!" Sal yelled, slamming his hand down on the counter. Bria jumped as their plates and silverware rattled.

Sal was breathing heavily and he smoothed his hand over his chest before running it through his hair. "You have every right to be mad at her and me and anyone you want, but I'm not gonna have you judge her. You didn't live her life. You didn't walk in her shoes. She made damn sure you didn't have to. And you know better than to curse in my home."

Maybe it was because Sal had never raised his voice with her. Maybe it was shock. Maybe it was the odd realization that her capable, assured mother had once been a mess. Whatever it was, Bria finally plucked up the nerve to ask the questions that had sat heavy on her tongue for her entire life.

"Why are you defending her? Why are you always on her side? You've loved her for forty years and she had another man's baby. A married man's baby! And you're still defending her. Why her?"

Sal walked around the kitchen island, pulled Bria from her stool, and hugged her.

Bria didn't think she was so close to tears, but as soon as she was safe in Sal's arms, she let go and cried her heart out on his chest. Sal held her until she was a sniveling mess. He used a kitchen towel to wipe her face like she was a small child, then smiled at her.

"Why not her?" he asked simply. "No one should have to be perfect to be loved. And for the record, I've never thought of you as another man's child. You've always been mine." He pulled her back into a hug and pressed a kiss to her forehead.

"I'm mad at her," Bria said, her face smushed against his chest.

"That's fine. Are you mad because she lied to you or because of who he was?"

"Because she lied," Bria said. "And because he was married."

"That makes sense. Do you want to know why she did what she did?"

"Yes."

"Then you'll have to ask her. You can tell her then that you're angry and why. Maybe it won't fix anything," he said, shrugging with her in his arms. "But it might."

"Okay," Bria said after a while.

"You know, considering the wild shit that happens in this town, it really doesn't make sense how dry the *Sentinel* is," Keith said out of the blue.

Bria turned toward her friend with a frown. "What a weird ass thing to say."

Keith rolled his eyes. "It was a general observation. Don't look at me like that. I'm not gonna call the *Sentinel* tip line and suggest they write about this. Anymore," he added hastily.

Bria hit him with the tear-stained kitchen towel while Sal laughed and grabbed a plate for his own breakfast.

WELCOME TO SEA PORT

TWENTY-TWO

Bria

On a normal day, the walk between Sal's apartment and home took ten minutes, twelve minutes max, but this morning Bria made sure it took twenty. She walked Keith home and stayed to talk with his mom about the chances of rain this week. Bria didn't care whatsoever, but she let Mrs. Lincoln talk for as long as she wanted.

Bria wasn't a fool. She knew as soon as they left Sal's house, he'd be on the phone with her mother before he even turned the lights on in the restaurant. So, she wasted time on the walk home, just to make her mother sweat. Eventually, even Mrs. Lincoln had other things to do and let Bria go, so she headed for home with yesterday's clothes in a plastic bag, her still-dead phone in the pocket of her sweatpants, and very slow steps.

Along the way, Bria ran into Mr. Worthington, her fifth grade English teacher, and Mrs. Worthington, her high school principal, and told them all about Confections' new teacake flavors. She stopped to watch a squirrel lug an acorn into a bush just for the hell of it. She even ran into Lorraine and Jonah nestled into the small alleyway behind the administrative building. They were all tangled up together but didn't seem put out when she stopped to say hey. They even waved hello as she passed. Well, Lorraine did. Bria quickened her steps before she found out where Jonah's hands were otherwise occupied; that was none of her business.

She wasted as much time as humanly possible in a town so small, but all too soon, she was standing in front of the white picket fence that surrounded her home with a pit in her stomach. She reached over the fence and played with the latch, wasting a bit more time before she let herself inside. Sal's crepes were churning in her gut but she knew she couldn't — wouldn't — put this off forever. Her mother hadn't raised her that way. The same mother who'd put off this conversation for far too long.

When she opened the door, she heard her mother in the kitchen. Bria stopped to toe off the spare pair of shoes she thankfully kept at Sal's and walked into the living room just as her mother did the same.

She was dressed in a coordinated sweatsuit set with an apron tied over her front. They stared at one another for a few silent moments before her mother broke the ice.

"You can yell at me if you want," she said. "But no cursing. Sal said you were cursing."

Classic Evelyn Stone.

Bria rolled her eyes. "It was one word."

"One word too many."

Bria started to say something smart but Sal's cautioning voice stayed her tongue. For the first time, maybe ever, Bria let go of the image of her mother she'd built as a little girl — someone who was larger than life and perfect. She was an adult now, so she tried to see Evelyn as a human being — as more than just the woman who birthed her. There were bags under Evelyn's eyes, she was wringing her hands, and the house smelled strongly of Pine-Sol and mustard greens. The unflappable Evelyn Stone was stress cleaning and cooking because of her.

"You made greens," Bria said.

"You hungry?"

Bria shook her head. "Sal made crepes and omelets."

Evelyn nodded and smoothed her palms over her apron.

"But I can eat a small bowl," Bria said.

Her mother's face lit up as she nodded. "Just a taste."

Bria dropped the plastic bag on the couch and followed her mother into the kitchen.

"Have a seat," Evelyn said as she pulled a bowl from the cabinet next to the sink. She moved to the large stockpot on the stove. The bowl was full to the brim when she set it in front of Bria and there was a fat chunk of pork on top, just the way Bria liked.

It was a small bowl by Evelyn's standards.

Bria wasn't hungry in the slightest, but Evelyn and Sal conveyed their love through food, so she ate a few bites while Evelyn watched her nervously. A few bites turned into half the bowl because Bria loved greens and no one knew that better than her mom.

"Well, I know you have questions," Evelyn said.

Bria nodded, setting the spoon back in her bowl.

"Go ahead. Ask me whatever you want."

Bria could see the nerves in her mother's body more than

her face. Her face was calm, blank even, but her hands were smoothing down her apron, organizing the salt and pepper shakers because when she was nervous or worried, her mom had to *do* things. Right now, apparently, she needed to make cornbread from scratch. They both knew Bria's great grandmother's cornbread recipe by heart.

Bria took one more taste of greens and wiped her mouth before she cleared her throat to speak. "Did he love you?"

Her mother was beating some eggs in a small bowl but her whisk stopped mid-stroke. That question caught her off guard. It caught Bria off guard as well.

"Why does that matter?" Evelyn asked, her tone curious rather than defensive.

Bria turned to look through the window above the kitchen sink. There wasn't much to see out there besides a clear blue sky, but she stared long enough to collect her thoughts.

Her mother was watching, but when Bria turned her attention back to the kitchen, Evelyn started whisking the eggs again.

"I don't care how he felt about me," Bria said in a small voice. "I accepted long ago that if my father, whoever he was, cared about me, he would've been in my life. He would have come back. Now I know he only had to walk across town, which proves my point."

Her mother's eyes were sad. She pressed her lips together, clearly trying not to frown, but she didn't correct Bria, which was answer enough.

"But it's one thing to know he didn't care about me and another to know that he never cared about you. I don't know why, but that's how I feel."

The thing Bria loved about her mom — the thing Keith often envied — was that her mother would listen to reason. She didn't invalidate her feelings because they conflicted with her own. She didn't talk down to her only child about important things. If Bria could explain herself, Evelyn would bend over backwards to validate her. Or, in this case, to answer a painful question.

"There was a moment when I thought he did, and I thought I loved him back." She took a breath and shook her head before she started speaking again. "But it was just a moment born out of hormones and foolishness. No, baby, he never loved me, and I don't think I ever loved him."

Hot tears fell down Bria's cheeks and she swiped them away, nodding sadly.

Her mother rushed to the paper towel holder by the sink and snatched one from the roll. She walked around the island and handed it to Bria, hovering close as she wiped her face.

"What's making you cry?"

Bria folded the paper towel and patted her cheeks. "Everyone wants to know they were created in love. Why wouldn't I cry about that?"

Evelyn sucked her teeth and smoothed one of Bria's twists behind her right ear. "That's not what you asked," she said. "You asked if he loved me and the answer is no. But I loved you. The moment I found out I was pregnant, all that foolishness went away. The hormones stayed, unfortunately, but nothing was more powerful than how much I loved you. And wanted you."

Bria let those words sink in, realizing she'd heard some version of this before.

Emboldened maybe, Evelyn kept speaking in a voice bright with happiness. "You were surrounded by love before you were anything more than a cluster of cells, actually. I loved you. Your grandparents loved you," she continued, referencing her mother and father who had always spoiled Bria as if she were the second coming of Jesus. "Sal loved you. Just because your biological father didn't love me or you doesn't mean that you weren't loved."

Evelyn's voice rose as she spoke, as if nothing made her more passionate than assuring her only daughter of this one fact.

Bria turned to her mother and found her eyes glassy with tears. "Why did you get with a married man of all people?" she asked. She recovered that question at the last second, stopping herself from opening the other secret between them, however obvious it was.

Evelyn collected herself for a few seconds before she answered. "Because I was young and bored. Because I didn't care about anyone else's feelings but my own. Because whatever you think about me now, I was a different person then. Having you made me want to become better."

"If you could go back—"

"I'd do it again," Evelyn said quickly, her voice strong and sure. She smoothed her hand over Bria's hair before walking back around the cabinet to finish mixing her cornbread. "What we did was mean and stupid, but it gave me you. I can have regrets, but I can't lie and say I'd do anything different because he gave me you." She finished with a shrug and then started folding the liquids into her cornmeal mixture.

"You don't have to lay it on so thick, mama. Is Sal one of

your regrets?" Bria whispered the question barely loud enough to be heard, but Evelyn's hand stilled again.

Evelyn and Sal had been best friends since childhood. Sometimes they joked as if they'd never been more than that — never wanted to be more than that — but everyone knew it was a lie, especially Bria. She'd had a front-row seat to their relationship for her entire life. She saw the way they looked at one another when they thought no one else could see, or when they thought Bria was too young to understand. The entire town talked about Sal loving Evelyn, but they never talked about how obvious it was that Evelyn loved him back.

Her mother's answer wasn't quick. She moved around the kitchen, collecting a baking pan and butter and stirring the batter a few more times just to have something to do. Bria didn't rush her. She watched as her mother scraped every drop of batter into the baking dish and slipped it into the oven. Evelyn took a deep breath before turning back to her with tears filling her eyes.

"When we were twelve, Sal asked me to marry him, and I said yes. We were kids and just playing. I thought we were playing, at least. I found out later that he was very serious. He asked me again when he turned seventeen two months after me. I told him no and broke his heart. I regret that for sure. And I regret how hurt he was when he found out about my relationship with the Mayor. But you know what I regret the most about that time?"

Bria shook her head, perched on the edge of her seat as she listened.

"I regret how goddamn happy he was when he found out I was pregnant. He shoved all his own hurts aside because he was so damn happy I was having a baby. I regret that I couldn't appreciate how loving he was until I'd already hurt him so bad. And when I tried to apologize, he wouldn't hear it." She laughed sadly. "That fool man just told me he'd never judge me and then gave me every cent of his savings to get me out of town."

"He told me."

"I bet he did. But did he tell you that he refused to talk to me about anything other than you for six months after I left?"

Bria shook her head. She couldn't remember a time when her mother and Sal went more than two days without talking. Well, except for when they were rooting for opposing basketball teams, but that was rare. No more than once every five years or so.

"Mmmhmm. Figured," Evelyn said. "I'd call and he'd pick up, but when I tried to ask how he was doing, he'd just shut down. When I talked about you, he had all the questions in the world. And every month, without fail, he sent me a care package. For you."

Bria didn't bother to wipe the tears from her cheeks. There were too many.

"He only started talking to me again because he realized it might be a little awkward to be in the delivery room without speaking to the person actually having the baby."

"God, mama, he really loves you."

"I know," Evelyn said. She picked up the mixing bowl and spoon and turned to the sink.

"Then why won't you tell him that you love him too?" Bria asked as she used the sleeves of her sweatshirt to wipe her eyes since the paper towel was soaked through.

There was a note of resigned sadness in Evelyn's voice.

"Because the last thing that man needs is to be saddled with me. He deserves better."

"Does he know that?" Bria mumbled.

Evelyn laughed but didn't answer.

Bria climbed from her stool and walked to her mother's side. "Sal said no one should have to be perfect to be loved."

"He would say something like that," Evelyn laughed.

"He would, and that's how I know you two deserve each other."

Her mother swallowed hard but didn't speak again. Bria wrapped her arms around her mother's shoulders and kissed her cheek. "Besides, you two already did all the hard stuff together. You raised me. Maybe you deserve a chance to do some of the good stuff too."

"Loving you was the best stuff," her mother said.

Bria sucked her teeth. "Says a woman who's been celibate for nearly three decades."

"Get out of my kitchen," Evelyn laughed, splashing Bria with water from the sink.

Bria ducked away, laughing herself. "I'm just sayin'," she replied.

"Say less," Evelyn said. "Much less."

Bria left her mother to finish stress cleaning and walked back to her bedroom. She still felt strange, but not nearly as sad as yesterday. The talk with her mother hadn't fixed much, but she thought they were on the right path.

There were other, far more terrifying conversations to come.

WELCOME TO SEA PORT

TWENTY-THREE

Willie

Willie had never felt alone in Sea Port. It was impossible. She was born and raised here. She knew every Portie, new and old. She was maybe the only person in town who could say that besides Knox. She knew every street and building intimately. That wasn't an exaggeration; it was Willie's job and also her birthright. How could she feel alone in a place where she was surrounded by dozens of people she knew well and who knew her?

But in the wake of these revelations about her family, she'd felt more alone than ever before, possibly from the hangovers, but also the sadness. She resolved in the hottest shower she could stand to rein herself in. She had to. If she wanted to keep her job, she probably shouldn't become one of Ms. Kemp's regulars.

She could hear Sully in her half of the duplex, stomping up and down the stairs. They'd had a few drinks last night but hadn't spoken. What was there to say? Willie had a sister and Sully was in love with her. Super awkward. So they decided to get drunk instead. And now they were both awake, hungover, and surly. It was hard for Willie not to blame herself for Sully's bad mood, but Willie had a tendency to blame herself for everything, so she took it all in stride as she dressed for the day and snuck out of the house like the coward she was.

Her calendar was clear, a rare blessing. After the last few days of difficult conversations, she wanted one day without having to speak to someone. She wanted one day to throw herself into the never-ending work of her position, even if it was only a distraction from the turmoil of her life.

She made a cup of tea at the hardly used coffee station in her office. At her desk, she unzipped her knee-high boots, stretched her feet, and opened the SPRI's application portal once again. She had a solid uninterrupted hour before someone was knocking at her door.

She lifted her gaze from her computer screen and glared at the hardwood. She desperately wanted to pretend not to be in, but no one who came knocking at her door was ever deterred by her silence. They knocked again, confirming her thoughts.

Willie sighed and stomped in her socks from her desk to the office door. Whoever was on the other side would just have to deal with it; she was too tired to be professional right now. She yanked the door open with force but then froze. She was expecting to find Santos and Knox on the other side, not Bria.

Definitely not Bria.

Over the last few weeks, Willie had developed a list of questions she was desperate to ask.

Do you have a long middle toe too?

Do you like to eat ice like our father did?

Do you prefer sour to sweet?

You know hypertension runs in our family, right?

But when presented with the opportunity to do so, she flubbed it. "What are you doing here?" she barked out.

Sully never would've let Willie live this moment down — Willie Waltham, political genius, disaster human being — so it was a good thing she wasn't here.

Bria's face fell and she started stuttering. "I— Sorry, I'm just... I know you're busy but I thought... I don't know. Sorry." She started to turn and Willie reached for her, a hand on the shoulder, which was surprisingly weird.

"No, fuck, I'm sorry. I'm just... I'm surprised to see you here," Willie said. "Do you want to come in?"

"Are you sure?" Bria asked, then her eyes dropped to Willie's socks.

Willie's gaze dropped too, shocked to find dancing jack-o-lanterns covering her feet. She didn't always wear seasonal themed socks — not anymore, at least, but they were a strange souvenir from another life, another place.

"They're comfortable," Willie said defensively. "Anyway, come in. Come in." She stepped back and made room for Bria to enter.

Bria eyed her office warily so Willie looked around as well, trying to see the room as Bria might — as a Waltham who didn't know this office like the back of their hand. She cringed at the state of her desk and rushed across the room to clear it up. She didn't want her first real conversation with her sister to happen over a stack of petitions.

"Sorry, sorry. Let me just..." She stifled the urge to

neaten the files and ruin her own organizational system. Instead, Willie set the papers on the couch in the neatest piles she could manage before ushering Bria into a chair on the other side of her desk.

"Have a seat," Willie said excitedly.

Bria sat gingerly, her knees pressed together and her face a nervous mask. Willie was stuck for a second as she tried to decide between sitting in her regular chair or on the other side of the desk. It was rare for her to be confused about how to behave in this office, but she eventually decided to take the chair next to Bria's.

She wanted a sister, not another constituent.

"So," Willie started, but then her brain froze. Willie could make small talk without even blinking. She could ask Bria how she'd been, what she thought about the weather, if she'd read the last edition of the *Sentinel* about Mr. Ford's haunted pumpkin patch, too late for Halloween but just in time for Thanksgiving. As the daughter of the former Mayor, Willie could small talk the town's church mothers under the table, but she didn't want to have small talk with Bria. Willie wanted to talk to Bria like a sister, but she didn't know her from Adam.

"Why Willie?" Bria asked into the silence.

"Why what?"

Bria smiled. "Why Willie? Why'd your parents name you Willie?"

"Oh." She smiled, more than adept at answering this question. "There's actually a long line of women named Willie in my mom's family. Willie Lee, Willie May, Willie Jo."

"So what are you?"

"Willie Ann," she replied. "I think it was supposed to be Willie Anna, but my mother thought the three syllables had a little more power."

Bria seemed to consider it for a second before a smile spread over her lips. "I like it. It's different."

"Well, what about you?" Willie asked. "How'd your mother come up with Bria?"

Bria smiled as if she, too, was used to answering this question. "It's Italian. It means vigor, liveliness."

"Okay," Willie breathed, smiling even though she wasn't sure that answered her question.

"Mama's been best friends with Sal Genova since forever so she gave her only child an Italian name." Bria smiled.

"Oh, okay. That's sweet."

"It strikes me more sad than sweet. Can you imagine being in love with someone for years — decades — and never being able to be with them?"

Willie tried not to frown because that was more information than she'd been expecting. She also didn't want to cry because she didn't have to imagine what that was like, unfortunately. So she steered the conversation back to safer ground. "Why are you here, Bria? I mean, I'm not mad, just...curious."

"Look," Bria started but didn't immediately continue. She was wringing her hands together but then pressed them to her thighs and started again. "So our parents were fucked up with how they handled all this."

Willie sighed in relief. "Very."

"But we don't have to keep that up," she said. "We can choose to be better."

"I agree. I've never thought about having a sister, but I'm open," she admitted.

"So am I!" Bria screeched. "I didn't mind being an only child."

"Same," Willie said. "But this could be...fun?"

"That's an option," Bria laughed.

It took a second for Willie to get what she meant and then she laughed as well. "The option I hope we choose. Even with all the...baggage between our families, I don't blame you."

Bria smiled. "I don't blame you either. I don't want to blame anyone, actually; I just want to get to know you." Bria's body relaxed after she said that, and Willie sighed knowingly.

"That's what I want too. And any questions you have about... I'll answer any questions you have."

Bria took in a few deep breaths before she answered. "If it's all right, I just want to get to know you right now. We can save some of the other stuff for later."

Willie nodded. "Absolutely. We'll take it slow." She and Bria smiled at each other, and even though she knew she probably shouldn't, she opened her mouth to ask the question sitting on the tip of her tongue. "Have you talked to Sully yet?"

Bria laughed softly and sighed. "Saving the best for last," she said. "No offense."

"None taken. I know she's great. Moody, but great."

"She's always been nice to me," Bria giggled, and Willie laughed with her sister.

There was a first time for everything.

SULLY

S ully was late for work again. Thankfully, Ani was on the schedule to open, or else a bunch of Sea Port caffeine addicts might have had a very bad morning.

She was tired, hungover, and the coffee shop's budget still wasn't finished.

She trudged into the café, made the strongest espresso she could manage, and then walked back to her cloffice without speaking more than two words to anyone. She'd texted Bria twice last night after a double bourbon and a shot of whisky. It had seemed like a good idea at the time and then a bad idea this morning, but it hardly mattered since Bria hadn't texted her back — she'd checked half a dozen times just on the walk from her house.

Frustration and sadness made it easier to finally get started on the budget and take her mind off, well...everything. She was so focused on the numbers that it took her a few seconds to realize the knocking she heard wasn't a migraine but someone literally knocking on her door.

"Come in," she called, pressing her fingers against her sore eyes. "What?" Sully asked when the door opened.

"Hi," Bria said.

Sully's mouth fell open in shock. "Hi. What are you doing here?"

Bria rolled her eyes. "You and Willie really need to work on your Southern hospitality."

"You talked to Willie?"

Bria smiled shyly. "I just came from her office, actually. She... We talked. She seems nice."

"She is."

"So you have good taste in people," Bria said, inching just inside the office. "Good to know." She was looking around surreptitiously, one eye on Sully, the other on the stack of lids in the corner.

"I like to think so," Sully replied. "So the talk with your... It went well?"

"You can say sister," Bria said, leaning her hip against Sully's desk.

Sully's fingers flinched on her keyboard as she thought about touching her. As she remembered the last time she'd touched Bria.

"And yeah, the talk went well."

"Good."

"We talked about you," Bria said.

"Why?"

Bria rolled her eyes and licked her lips. "'Cause she loves you and wants to see you happy. And apparently, she's under the impression that I make you happy."

Sully had already given up on finishing the budget today once she saw Bria, but now she saved her progress and closed the spreadsheet entirely, sitting back in her chair. "She does know me better than anyone."

Bria's eyes wandered over Sully's chest and she licked her lips again. "For now," she whispered.

It took every ounce of restraint Sully had not to pull Bria

into her lap. Not yet. She stood from her desk and closed the door. Bria sat on the desk and lifted her chin to look at Sully with nothing but heat in her eyes.

"I know you've got more important stuff to deal with, but I owe you an apology."

Bria blinked a few times. "For what?"

"For not telling you about Willie and your...parents when I found out. I couldn't... Willie's my best friend and she was messed up about it and about us. It was a lot all at once."

"It was. Is," Bria corrected. "But it wasn't your place. This isn't your baggage."

"It's not," Sully whispered. "But I want you to know that I wanted to tell you. I wanted to be there for you."

Bria's smile returned. "Willie said you'd say something like that."

"Okay."

"And like I said, this isn't your baggage. It's mine. I just hope you won't decide not to date me just because my family is a plot from a low-budget soap opera during sweeps."

Sully stepped forward and tentatively pressed her hands on either side of Bria's waist. They both sucked in a harsh breath. "My family's more like a double episode of a criminal procedural. I won't judge you if you won't judge me."

Bria's eyes went wide. "I don't want to derail this conversation, but you better believe I'm gonna ask *all* the questions when I get the chance."

Sully laughed gently. "That's fine. I'm used to it."

"Sea Port is getting so interesting these days," Bria said, grabbing Sully by the shoulders and pulling her close.

"Is it?" Sully asked, dipping her head, her mouth hovering over Bria's.

"Very. I mean, between the Lorraine and Jonah sightings alone, this place is so much cooler than it's ever been."

Sully kissed the corner of her mouth. "Do you really think they're exhibitionists?" she breathed against Bria's bottom lip.

Bria licked Sully's question from her mouth and then lifted her head to kiss her lightly. "Absolutely, but who am I to judge? Under the right circumstances, I could be as well."

"Right circumstances?" Sully asked. Their lips touched as she spoke.

"You," Bria whispered into Sully's mouth as Sully's tongue slid along the seam of Bria's lips. "I'd do damn near anything to taste you again."

They locked the office door, not that it mattered. The room was so small and the walls were so thin that anyone in the back room could probably hear them, Sully just didn't care. She wanted to be with Bria and refused to wait any longer.

Sully cupped Bria's breasts through her t-shirt while Bria slowly unbuckled Sully's pants. They kissed one another in small sips, tasting and teasing each other with an all-consuming focus. It had barely been a full day since they'd last been together but they touched one another like it had been months.

Sully moved her hands under Bria's shirt and played with her hard nipples while Bria shoved her left hand into Sully's pants. They kissed one another around laughter and smiles and moans.

All the turmoil of the last few days melting away as they touched.

WELCOME TO SEA PORT

Epilogue
BRIA

Two weeks later...

Bria hadn't technically moved in with Sully, she just slept at her house at least three nights a week. So not like most of the time, but a lot. Sully had graciously cleared out a drawer for some of Bria's clothes and that was how they got into this predicament.

"Hmm." Bria scratched her head at what she saw inside Sully's bottom drawer.

"We don't have to use all of this," Sully said. "I mean, obviously. But I can get rid of whatever you don't like." Sully's voice shook with every second word, her anxiety growing while Bria continued to stare at her impressive collection of sex toys.

"I mean, *obviously*," Bria said contemplatively. "But I don't think we should be hasty with our decision."

"What?" Sully breathed.

Bria couldn't contain her smile any longer. "I'm saying

we should try everything before we make any decisions. How else will we know if we like something if we don't try it?"

They were both giggling by the time Bria was done speaking. "I can't believe you're just now letting me see all this!"

"I wasn't sure if you'd..."

"I would," Bria said, grabbing a bright red dildo at the top of the pile. She held it in one hand and waved it at Sully. "Would you?"

Sully snatched a harness from the drawer and showed Bria. "I would," Sully breathed.

Bria crawled onto the bed and smiled over her shoulder, her bare butt pointing right at her as she tipped her hips left to right. "Then let's go."

Sully bent over and playfully bit Bria's left butt cheek, then slapped her ass lightly. Bria giggled at the loud crack of skin-on-skin and then moaned when Sully licked her crack.

Bria had never been particularly sentimental, but she wanted to etch every minute of this night on her heart. She crawled onto her stomach and crossed her ankles, giving Sully her full attention while she stepped into the harness. She licked her lips at the sight of Sully's fingers gliding over the black leather and cold metal. She squeezed her thighs together when Sully pulled the buckles on either side of her hips tight, securing it to her body with a soft inhale. And she moved her hand between her legs as Sully rubbed lubrication onto the dildo once it was seated in place.

Bria sat up on her knees on the bed and pulled Sully's face to hers. The kiss wasn't tender, it was desperate and full of longing. Bria knew she and Sully were moving quickly. Even if everything she thought she knew about her life hadn't recently imploded, less than a month was too soon to tell Sully she loved her.

Wasn't it?

But even if she didn't say it, Bria felt it.

She pulled Sully on top of her and kissed her slow and deep. It was as close to the words as she could get.

"You're so beautiful," Sully mumbled in between kisses and licks at Bria's mouth.

Bria opened her legs, sighing when she felt Sully's fingers glance over her clit and then at her opening. She felt the soft head of the dildo pressing at her sex and moaned loudly.

"Tell me if it feels weird," Sully said as she moved the dildo up and down Bria's lips.

"Please," was all Bria could think to whisper, her voice tight with need. "Please."

They held each other's gaze as Sully pushed slowly inside. Her hand brushed Bria's sex, rubbed soft circles over her clit. She moaned. Sully's hips stilled as she let Bria adjust.

"Please," Bria whined again.

Sully raised her hand to lick her thumb and Bria held her breath until that wet digit pressed against her clit. They started rocking together in a slow, torturous, and loving rhythm.

"I love you," Bria sighed just before she came.

She didn't care if they were moving fast. If the recent upheaval in her life had taught her anything, it was that life was too short to let a single happy moment go to waste.

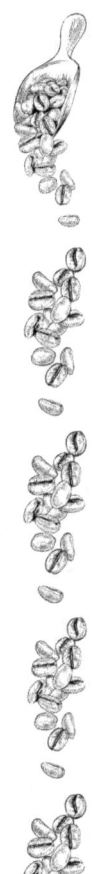

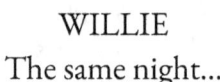

WILLIE
The same night...

One second, she was pressing send on the latest batch of relocation acceptances and the next, her brain was wandering.

"Nope," she said, mentally yanking herself back on track.

After weeks of drama, she was finally starting to feel like herself again. Well, a version of herself — a version who still loved tea but wasn't speaking to her mother — but more like herself than before. She was sleeping better and finally starting to dig herself out of the backlog of work that had piled up while she was basically stalking Bria. She was better now, and there was so much to do!

Now that the latest round of Transplants was hopefully on the way, Willie turned to the next item on her never-ending to-do list. She grabbed the red folder next to her office phone, stuffed with various handwritten complaints from one old Portie or another — all somehow about the influx of new people. Most of the complaints amounted to an accusation that the Transplants were disrupting the town's way of life. Whatever that meant.

"Never mind," she said, hiding the folder behind her phone. It had been a good day in a great week; Willie didn't want to ruin her mood for something that could easily be put off to tomorrow, so she grabbed the green folder instead. This folder had a financial audit of the town's viability, and it was not great. Not great at all. Like most small towns in the country if not the world, Sea Port lived right on the precipice of dissolution. Or at least, that had been the case when Willie had been elected. The very first thing on her list as the new mayor of Sea Port had been to apply for a Global Good Fund grant, earmarked specifically for small towns and villages with fresh plans to save themselves.

Willie's plan to entice new blood to Sea Port wasn't original — there had been programs like it all over North America and Europe — but Willie didn't think it was necessary to reinvent the wheel to have a good idea. That's why she took on the population revitalization scheme, with plans for modernization projects and historic preservation to come. The latter had been on hold as she'd applied for more funding to preserve the crumbling historical landmarks littered around town. The best she'd been able to do with Jonah Brown's help was to close down the buildings they couldn't renovate just yet.

But now it was time for the second phase of Sea Port's revival. The old financial audit served as a reminder of all she'd done for the town, stories she could use for her campaign to keep the job that still felt like her father's. She was running unopposed, but Skip Waltham's first rule of politics was to never get too comfortable.

Comfort bred laziness, laziness bred failure, and Walthams never failed.

He might not have been the husband she thought he was, but she was still Skip Waltham's daughter.

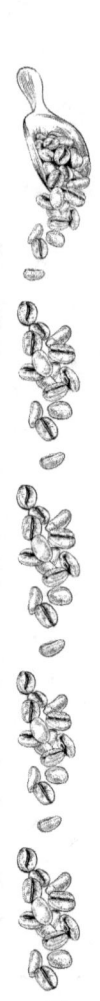

Also by Katrina Jackson

Welcome to Sea Port

From Scratch

Inheritance

Small Town Secrets

Her Christmas Cookie

The Spies Who Loved Her

Pink Slip

Private Eye

Bang & Burn

New Year, New We

His Only Valentine

Bright Lights

Honey Pot

Erotic Accommodations

Room for Three?

Neighborly

Love At Last

Every New Year

One More Valentine

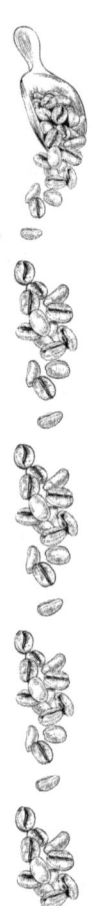

Heist Holidays
Grand Theft N.Y.E.

The Family
Beautiful and Dirty

The Hitman

The Enforcer

Dolci

The Don

Dolore

Bay Area Blues
Layover

Back in the Day

Curriculum Vitae
Office Hours

Sabbatical

Mosley Coven
The Night Gate (website exclusive)

A Flicker to a Flame

Invocation

-

<u>Standalone stories</u>

Encore

The Tenant

Sex Toy Soldier

Looking

And When You Leave Me

Small Mercies